SPECIAL MESSAGE TO READERS

This book is published under the auspices of

THE ULVERSCROFT FOUNDATION

(registered charity No. 264873 UK)

Established in 1972 to provide funds for research, diagnosis and treatment of eye diseases. Examples of contributions made are: —

A new Children's Assessment Unit at Moorfield's Hospital, London.

•

Twin operating theatres at the Western Ophthalmic Hospital, London.

•

A Chair of Ophthalmology at the University of Leicester.

•

The establishment of a Royal Australian College of Ophthalmologists "Fellowship".

You can help further the work of thc Foundation by making a donation or leaving a legacy. Every contribution, no matter how small, is received with gratitude. Please write for details to:

THE ULVERSCROFT FOUNDATION,
The Green, Bradgate Road, Anstey,
Leicester LE7 7FU, England.
Telephone: (0116) 236 4325

In Australia write to:
THE ULVERSCROFT FOUNDATION,
c/o The Royal Australian College of Ophthalmologists,
27, Commonwealth Street, Sydney, N.S.W. 2010.

Love is
a time of enchantment:
in it all days are fair and all fields
green. Youth is blest by it,
old age made benign:
the eyes of love see
roses blooming in December,
and sunshine through rain. Verily
is the time of true-love
a time of enchantment — and
Oh! how eager is woman
to be bewitched!

MASQUERADE OF VENGEANCE

Years of exile in an Australian convict settlement fuelled his passion for revenge against three men. Now the day of reckoning was at hand . . . Sir Eustace Knowle was found battered to death. Threatening, anonymous letters had already been delivered to two others in the party gathered for the wedding of Sir George Marton's daughter. A chain of mysterious events and frightening 'accidents' followed. It was at the masked ball that the Honourable Justin Rutherford and his niece, Anthea, witnessed the first incident — but this seemed an unlikely start to one of their famous adventures . . .

Books by Alice Chetwynd Ley in the Ulverscroft Large Print Series:

THE JEWELLED SNUFF BOX
A CONFORMABLE WIFE
THE GEORGIAN RAKE
THE MASTER OF LIVERSEDGE
AT DARK OF THE MOON

ALICE CHETWYND LEY

MASQUERADE OF VENGEANCE

Complete and Unabridged

ULVERSCROFT
Leicester

First published in Great Britain in 1989

First Large Print Edition
published 1996

British Library CIP Data

Ley, Alice Chetwynd, *1913* –
Masquerade of vengeance.—Large print ed.—
Ulverscroft large print series: romance
1. English fiction—20th century
2. Large type books
I. Title
823.9′14 [F]

ISBN 0–7089–3653–9

Published by
F. A. Thorpe (Publishing) Ltd.
Anstey, Leicestershire

Set by Words & Graphics Ltd.
Anstey, Leicestershire
Printed and bound in Great Britain by
T. J. Press (Padstow) Ltd., Padstow, Cornwall

This book is printed on acid-free paper

For my dear grandson James,
who thought it was about time

1

THERE had been no moon, but now, towards dawn, a thin grey line on the horizon just distinguished the sky from the dark swell of the ocean. The waves slapped against the sides of the boat as the men bent their backs to the oars, sending their craft running through the water towards a paler line of foam which fringed the shore.

Only one man did not row. He sat immobile, his body taut, staring with unfocused eyes at the solid dark rise of the cliffs sheltering the beach.

He was here at last, back once more in his native land. Not that it had ever done anything for him, other than to banish him into exile. His lips tightened as he recalled those brutish early years; the months in irons, working like an animal in the bush, the treadmill and the lash. He might have died under the harsh rule — many had — before he at last gained his 'ticket of leave' and the easier times that went with it.

He could have remained there then, all those thousands of miles away from these shores, working in the service of one of the wealthy farmers until he had risen to a position of some authority, even to the ownership of his own land. He knew himself to be capable enough.

But always the passion for revenge drove him on to return to England and seek out those who, however small a part they had played, in his view were responsible for his downfall. Three men there were, who in different ways had been culpable. Wherever they might be now, let them look out for themselves! They should die, certainly, and no swift death. No, they should learn the meaning of apprehension and fear even as he had been forced to do. This he had sworn many times over in the years of suffering.

The day of reckoning was at hand.

* * *

His first sight of London took him aback. After so many years, he had forgotten the noise and bustle of the City at the start of a new day, so different from the quiet and decorum of the fashionable West End.

Brewers' drays and carts, up from the country with hay for the London markets, clattered over the cobblestones, while drovers skilfully guided herds of sheep and cattle towards Smithfield. Clerks hurried along the pavements to their counting houses, trying to avoid the tradesmen who were taking down the shutters from their shops and sweeping the steps in readiness for another day's trade. He was jostled by these and a host of others; chimney sweeps carrying brushes, milkmaids with pails suspended on a yoke from their shoulders, scarlet coated postmen ringing their bells as they delivered the early mail — all intent on their business and caring nothing for loiterers.

He had not forgotten his way to his one-time refuge, however, in a sleazy quarter not far from the magnificence of St Paul's Cathedral. He had been told by other criminals that nothing had changed here. The landlord of the Red

Lion in Fleet Market had grown heavier with the years, but he was still an incurious individual, this attitude being best suited to his specialised trade. He failed to recognise the newcomer, a fact which satisfied one who had been a regular customer of his in the distant past. The correct signals were given, however, so there was no difficulty in obtaining admission.

The man did not linger there, but having transacted his business, moved on to a modest though respectable coffee house in the Strand. He emerged from this some time later, having changed his clothes for more fashionable attire.

Thus clad, he took a hackney to Stratton Street, Piccadilly, where he dismounted and knocked upon a door. It was opened by a dark-suited individual with the look of a gentleman's gentleman.

The visitor mentioned a name, and asked if its owner was within. He was met with a hostile look.

"I fear not. *That* gentleman quit my rooms several years since, and a good riddance, I must say! No one has inquired for him since I don't know when," he added, disdainfully. "Then it was mostly men dunning. If you're on the same errand, you'll catch cold at it."

He prepared to close the door, but the visitor swiftly interposed a foot.

"One moment," he said, cajolingly. "Could you be so vastly obliging as to furnish me with his direction?"

The man hesitated, for the visitor appeared to be a person of some standing. Then he stiffened.

"No, I couldn't, for I don't know it!" he snapped. "And be good enough to shift your foot!"

The visitor complied, and the door slammed in his face.

He shrugged. Maybe it was not going to be as easy as he had hoped. After all, it was a long time . . .

Very well, he would seek out the others. At least he was tolerably certain where they might be found. There was just a chance that they, too, might be in London, as they had always had a town-house in Cavendish Square. They would lead him to the first object of his revenge, but they should not escape themselves. No, nor that other, though he was of lesser importance. Everyone concerned must pay the price.

His jaw was set grimly as he hailed another hackney.

Several hours later, he was boarding the mail coach for York.

* * *

Sir Nathaniel Conant was chief magistrate of the renowned Bow Street police office founded by the novelist Henry Fielding some sixty years before, and later expanded by his half brother Sir John Fielding, known as the Blind Beak. It was the foremost in importance of the seven other police offices later set up by a reluctant government, and the only one to be permitted to send officers — known as Runners — into the country to pursue investigations.

Sir Nathaniel looked speculatively at the man standing erect before him in the manner of an ex-soldier, which indeed he was. Runner Joseph Watts was one of his best officers; the jutting jaw indicated his tenacity of purpose, and the long, sharp nose suggested the curiosity which was a hallmark of the good detective.

'He will do,' thought the magistrate, nodding, and aloud, he said, "I understand, Watts, that you're not engaged in an inquiry at present?"

"No, sir. It's been quiet of late for me, ever since the Jermyn case."

"Ah, yes." Conant did not need reminding of the extraordinary affair concerning the late Sir Aubrey Jermyn[1]. It had caused quite a stir at the time, involving as it did a member of the Prince Regent's circle. The investigation had also received assistance from an unorthodox source, another member of the Quality.

The Honourable Justin Rutherford, youngest brother of Viscount Rutherford, had the reputation of being a notable academic with antiquarian interests. He was also a young man intrigued by any kind of puzzle, and had lately been turning his hand to amateur detection. His association with Joseph Watts had begun during a brief period a few years

---

1 *vide* A FATAL ASSIGNATION

earlier when Captain Rutherford had been on Wellington's staff in the Peninsula as an intelligence officer, and Watts had served under him.

"The authorities in York," continued Sir Nathaniel, "are concerned about a number of jewel robberies which have occurred of late in the town and surrounding district. There is to be an important masked ball at the Assembly Rooms shortly, so our assistance has been requested."

He paused.

"They asked for Townsend," he continued. "But you know how it is — he's in Brighton attending the Prince Regent at this time of year. The man can't be everywhere at once. Of course, it's the name."

Watts nodded. John Townsend was the senior Runner at Bow Street. He had served there for nearly thirty years and had the important task of safeguarding the royal family. He was also employed by the Bank of England on dividend days, when large sums of money were handled. His reputation meant that his presence was frequently requested at fashionable parties; when the words 'Mr Townsend will attend' were inscribed on the invitation cards, guests might feel secure. Townsend knew the 'swell mob', and they knew it was wise to avoid him.

"Nevertheless, if the presence of a Bow Street Runner is announced, that should act as a sufficient deterrent," said Sir Nathaniel in conclusion. "They offer generous terms and accommodation at the Old Starre in Stonegate. A pleasant assignment, I should think — almost a holiday, in fact."

2

EVERYONE was agreed that the wedding at Firsdale Hall, the residence of Sir George and Lady Marton situated a few miles outside York, had been a prodigious success. The female members of the household staff, from the humblest kitchen-maid to the stately housekeeper, thought that no bride could have looked lovelier than Miss Marianne in her gown of cream silk, trimmed with Mechlin lace. As for the three bridesmaids — Marianne's younger sister Frances, still in the schoolroom, and her two cousins, the Honourable Anthea Rutherford and Miss Louisa Harvey — they had presented a picture which even the least impressionable male present had allowed was charming. Several of the *more* impressionable went further, declaring themselves to be quite bowled over by one or other of the two elder bridesmaids.

The wedding had naturally been

attended by a host of people — family, friends and neighbours; for Firsdale Hall had been in the possession of Sir George Marton's forbears during the past three hundred years. Some of the guests, mostly family, had travelled long distances to attend, so were staying at the Hall.

"And I do beg you," Lady Marton had said several days before the ceremony, "not to desert us and all return home as soon as the wedding is over! It will seem so odiously flat with everyone gone and the house to all intents and purposes empty! Poor George and I will be moped to death — not to mention dear Fanny!"

Poor George, a somewhat portly gentleman in his late forties with the tanned complexion of an out-doors man, looked surprised at this remark, but did not refute it.

Lady Marton's eldest brother, Viscount Rutherford, laughed.

"I believe George will survive, eh, old fellow? But as you know, Julia, Elizabeth and I have arranged to go on from here for a tour of the Lakes. Anthea doesn't especially wish to come with us, but I don't know — "

He broke off, looking doubtfully at his daughter. Anthea Rutherford was a girl of nineteen with a piquant, lively face, hazel eyes which often glinted with mischief, and a Titus crop of dark curls. She had a trick of deciding matters for herself.

"Now, do say *you'll* stay, Anthea," begged her aunt. "Poor Fanny will be quite desolate — she's going to miss Marianne, you know, in spite of having our neighbour's daughter Anne de Ryde always looking in, with her governess. She'll need to become accustomed to the lack of an elder sister's company at home, I know, but just at first it would soften the parting if you were to stay for a while. Louisa — " her tone sounded less eager — "says she will stay on if you do. And as Harry intends to remain here for the Races, she will have her brother to escort her home. If you don't wish to accompany your parents to the Lakes, it would be the very thing!"

"Indeed, it would be convenient," put in Anthea's mother, "besides being most agreeable, of course," she added, hastily. "We could call here on our way back to Town and take you up."

She looked anxiously at her daughter as she spoke, and was quite relieved when Anthea graciously accepted the invitation. She reflected that at least she could now be sure that the girl would not be getting up to any of her mad starts in her parents' absence.

She should have known better. One could never be sure of anything where Anthea was concerned.

Lady Marton was already aware of this, and ventured a word of advice to her sister-in-law after the wedding was over, and the Rutherfords were about to set off for the Lakes.

"You know, Elizabeth," she began, in a firm tone, "it's high time that Anthea was married."

Lady Rutherford smiled indulgently. "Oh, yes, *we* are quite persuaded of that, my dear Julia. The thing is, how to persuade Anthea?"

"Well, you don't mean to tell me she lacks for suitors," protested her hostess. "Why, wherever she goes there are men surrounding her! Surely there must be someone of them who takes her fancy?"

"Not seriously, I fear. She takes up

with first one beau, then another! I've quite given up hope of ever seeing it come to anything, though at first I was on tenterhooks, thinking each one would be Mr Right at last."

"One needs to make a little push in these matters," replied Julia, with the confidence of a mother who had recently managed to get a daughter wed. "Now tell me, my dear, what do you say to Mr Rogers?"

"Can you mean Sprog?" asked Lady Rutherford.

"Such an ugly nickname," deprecated Julia Marton. "Just the kind of sobriquet that schoolboys delight in foisting on each other, and unfortunately it often remains with them for the rest of their lives."

"True. I do remember not to call him by it to his face — at least, most of the time. But I'm so accustomed to hearing Justin use it, that I fear it does slip out sometimes," confessed Lady Rutherford.

"Yes, yes, I understand that," replied Julia Marton, a shade impatiently. "But you haven't answered my question, Elizabeth — what *do* you think of him as a husband for Anthea? His parents and ours were close friends — I mean my parents, the Rutherfords, of course, and not George's. Moreover, Mr Rogers and Justin were at school and Oxford together; always the best of friends, too. Would you approve of a match there?"

Lady Rutherford smiled. "Indeed I would! So, too, would Justin and Ned — " she referred to her husband Edward, Viscount Rutherford. "Nothing would please them more than to see Sidney Paul Rogers a member of the family. He's not only a delightful young man, but of course a most eligible *parti*, well connected and so on. But — "

"Precisely," cut in Julia, sweeping aside this hint of a possible objection. "He's so eligible, my dear Elizabeth, that I am of the firm opinion that there must be dozens of hopeful mamas on the catch for him for their daughters! Which is why I made sure that both he and Anthea would be staying here in the house for the wedding, and not to have him putting up at an hotel in York. He's agreed to stay on for a while, too, in order to accompany Justin on some of those peculiar antiquarian expeditions of his, so that should be splendid, don't you agree?"

"Well, yes," responded her sister-in-law doubtfully. "That's to say, yes, of course," she added in a livelier tone, seeing Julia's somewhat crestfallen face. "It's vastly good of you, my dear Julia, to go to so much trouble."

The doubts Lady Rutherford could not help feeling would have been increased could she have been privileged to hear a conversation between her brother-in-law Justin and his niece Anthea on this very same subject.

The pair were on very easy terms, more like brother and sister than uncle and niece. This was scarcely surprising with only fourteen years difference in age, and a strong similarity of temperament. Justin was frequently in and out of his brother's town house in Berkeley Square whenever he chanced to be in London, although he had a snug set of bachelor rooms in Albemarle Street.

"You know, Justin," said Anthea, solemnly, but with an irrepressible twinkle in her eye, "I have the most melancholy persuasion that my aunt, not content with having married off Marianne, is determined to perform the same office for me."

"No, you don't say? Whatever gives you that notion, my dear niece?"

"As if you didn't know," she retorted. "Your much vaunted powers of deduction must be in abeyance at present!"

"Well, a fellow can't always be exercising his undoubted talents," replied Justin, loftily. "Besides," he continued, grinning, "only a fool would attempt to make any accurate deductions from the behaviour of a female."

Anthea inspected him as if he were something nasty which had just crawled out of a garden vegetable.

"Females, of course, being so vastly inferior — a lesser breed, in fact?"

"We — ell — "

He dodged a flying cushion.

"At least there's one thing you must allow they can't do," he said, reasonably. "And that's to aim straight."

"You're the greatest beast in Nature," she informed him, but without rancour.

"And you're regrettably wanting in

conduct, let me tell you. Suppose anyone had chanced to come in at that moment? A gently-reared female pelting people with cushions! I ask you!"

"You're not people, and, of course, I don't make a habit of it."

"You relieve my mind," he said, mockingly. "But tell me, niece, what leads you to suspect that Aunt Julia's planning to push *you* into Parson's Mousetrap? Why not Louisa, for instance?"

"Oh, surely you've heard that Louisa is as good as engaged? You must have noticed how particular Aunt Julia is to thrust me into the company of your friend Mr Rogers! It's as plain as a pikestaff. Apart from that, she went to such lengths to urge him to stay on after the wedding."

"Hm. As I recall, she pressed all of us, you and myself included."

"Pray do not be so obtuse! We are family, so it's natural she should press us to stay on."

"Equally natural that she should invite Sprog, seeing that he and I are old friends who rarely get the chance to be in company together nowadays."

"Oh, yes, I dare say, but all the same I think she means to be matchmaking," insisted Anthea. "A female can sense such things. But I can tell you she'll catch cold at *that*," she finished, emphatically.

Justin's dark eyes held a twinkle. "But why, dear niece? One supposes you must wed sometime, and Sprog's a splendid fellow, I assure you."

"I don't doubt it, but I will not have him — or anyone else for that matter — thrust upon me! I shall choose my own husband, if and when I decide to take one!"

"An admirable scheme. And, of course, one must consider the fact that my friend may take a similar stand." Justin's smile was provocative. "Irresistible as you undoubtedly are to most men, my dear Anthea, there's no saying that you appear so to Sprog. Always a fellow with a mind of his own, don't you know?"

"Oh, you — !"

Her indignation turned to laughter, in which Justin joined.

"Well, I can readily undertake to keep him out of your way for most of the time," he said, at last. "He's as keen as mustard to accompany me to some of the historic sites hereabouts. Yorkshire's a capital county for mediaeval buildings: castles, monastic houses, churches — in fact, worthy of a book on its own. Although, as you know, I'd intended to make a wider survey of English antiquities in general."

Anthea nodded. She was well aware of her uncle's reputation in the academic world, based on a book he had had published some years earlier dealing with the antiquities of Greece. But he was no dry-as-dust scholar. A keen sportsman, a notable whip, and — when the spirit moved him — a lively participant in social occasions; he could fit into most company.

"Do you mean to go to the Lord Mayor's masquerade in costume?" she asked, changing the subject.

"I don't mean to go at all," he said, with a grimace.

"Oh, that's too bad of you! I was counting on your escort."

"You'll have your aunt and uncle besides Louisa and Harry — what more do you want? Of course, I dare say Sprog could be prevailed upon to escort you."

As the gentleman in question entered the room at that moment, she was prevented from replying.

Sidney Paul Rogers was in his early thirties, with rich auburn hair, intelligent grey eyes and an open, friendly expression. His buff pantaloons, a blue coat closely fitting his broad shoulders, and an intricately tied neckcloth, all indicated the man of fashion; but he had an easy, casual way of wearing these garments which dispelled any suggestion of the dandy.

He greeted Anthea with a slight bow and a warm smile which she answered with a roguish look.

"Did I hear you speaking of the masquerade, Miss Anthea?" he asked.

"You've been eavesdropping!" she accused, blushing a little in spite of herself because of Justin's last remark. "How monstrous of you!"

"No such thing, ma'am. The door was open, so I paused a moment on the threshold, admiring — if I may say so — the delightful picture you present in that gown," he answered, promptly.

Her eyes sparkled with merriment, but she tried to look severe.

"Bah! You're quite shameless, and I don't believe a word of it!"

"I assure you," he insisted, his grey eyes serious for a moment.

Justin, observing this scene with amusement, saw fit to interrupt it. He coughed delicately.

"Now that you two have exchanged the civilities," he said, with a grin, "you may as well admit the soft impeachment, Anthea. She was quizzing me to escort her to the masquerade at the Assembly Rooms tomorrow."

"Could you possibly think of refusing?" asked Mr Rogers, incredulously. "How shabby! But I think one must admit that it's typical." He turned to Anthea again. "I know it's a poor substitute, but may I offer myself in Justin's place?"

She looked confused for a moment.

"No need to," put in Justin, deftly. "I'll be going, too. My sister has tickets for us all, so unfortunately she'll require it. I was only teasing you, Anthea."

* * *

Sir George Marton, like his grandfather and father before him, was a Justice of the Peace. He did not find the duties too onerous. Most local crime was confined to minor misdemeanours he could deal with himself, without reference to his fellow magistrates in the county. Slightly more serious offences were dealt with when the local magistrates met at Petty sessions; while felonies, the most serious of all, were referred to a high court before a jury. Occasionally preliminary investigation into cases of felony would require him to have witnesses brought before him for questioning, but such instances were rare. When they did arise, he performed his task diligently, issuing warrants for a search and for arrest as necessary. In cases of riot, he would have been in charge both of individual citizens and the officers of any troops sent to deal with the disturbance. Fortunately, nothing of that kind ever came his way. The humble residents of Firsdale and its surrounding villages were not given to riotous assembly.

This was a system which had persisted since the Middle Ages and it was still satisfactory in rural areas. Sir George and Lady Marton were well liked and looked up to in their neighbourhood. His tenants were not afraid to bring their grievances to his land agent Hutton, knowing that most often Squire himself would deal with them. He was judged a fair man, but a shrewd one whom it was no use trying to humbug.

So it was with a feeling of outrage that he read the letter which had arrived on his desk in the library with the rest of his morning post.

It was both offensive and threatening. Moreover, with increasing disgust, he saw that it was also anonymous.

His first instinct was to tear it into shreds, but his magisterial habits restrained him. Someone was responsible for this; and, by God, he meant to know who it was. It was written in capitals, so offered no clue.

He pulled the bell rope, and his butler entered the room promptly. There had been something peremptory about the summons.

"Yes, Sir George?"

"This letter, Oldroyd," said his master

abruptly, holding out the missive cover side up. "Did someone collect it with the others from the receiving office this morning?"

Oldroyd looked from the letter to Sir George's face. He knew that expression, and it bode ill for somebody.

"Yes, Sir George. One of the footmen went — Will, I think it was. Should I enquire, sir?"

"Do, and send Will to me, if indeed it was Will."

"Very good, sir."

Oldroyd withdrew, and presently a young and slightly scared footman appeared. In answer to his master's question, he said that he had collected all the post for the Hall as usual from Ned Appleton at the village post office. He waited in some trepidation for Sir George's reaction to this news, then sighed with relief when he was dismissed.

Sir George pondered for a moment, frowning. The letter bore no postmark, therefore could not have gone through the usual official channels. It would not do to make too much of a stir about it, villages being hotbeds of gossip; but he meant to have a quiet word with Ned Appleton to try and discover how the fellow had come by it. Meanwhile, he tossed it contemptuously into a drawer of his desk.

As things turned out, he was unable to stroll down to the village that morning to pursue his inquiries, and he very soon forgot the matter in the household bustle going on over the Lord Mayor's masquerade to be held at the Assembly Rooms that evening. All the younger members of the family were to attend, attired in historical or fancy costumes which had just been delivered by carrier from York. As is frequent with hired costumes, none of these fitted their prospective wearers satisfactorily. There was much trying on, altering and trying on again, with demands from each to the others to say if the latest alteration seemed to be better or not. Partly exasperated, partly amused, he tried to steer clear of involvement with what he firmly announced was female business, only to be thwarted by his wife and daughter

Fanny, who both insisted on seeking his opinion.

Being only sixteen and therefore not yet out, Fanny could not be present at the masquerade. Instead, she was to have her friend Anne de Ryde to keep her company for the evening in the chaperonage of Anne's governess. This did not prevent Fanny from taking the liveliest interest in the costumes to be worn by her cousins Anthea and Louisa, and in seconding her mama in offering opinions and advice to these two young ladies.

Louisa Harvey had chosen the costume of a Puritan maid — a style suited to her somewhat demure looks. This would not do for Anthea, who, after having been sternly forbidden by her aunt to wear a scanty garb intended to represent Diana the Huntress, had finally settled upon that of Cleopatra.

Justin had helpfully informed her that she could use her imagination to the full, as there was no portrait extant of Egypt's renowned Queen, so Shakespeare's description must be her only guide.

"And just as well if she don't model her attire too closely on authentic sources," he confided privately to Rogers and young Harry Harvey, "judging from the ancient Egyptian tomb paintings I've seen of females in transparent robes!"

Her aunt could find nothing to scandalise her in the result of Anthea's efforts; although she cast a wary eye over them. The girl certainly looked lovely in a clinging white linen gown with broad satin sash of lapis lazuli colour fastened round her waist by a gold clasp of Egyptian design. Her dark curls were crowned by a gold band ornamented with a hooded cobra, the royal emblem of the Pharaohs.

Sidney Rogers, attired as a dashing cavalier in rich red satin with lace-edged collar and cuffs, and a hat trimmed with an enormous plume, obviously found difficulty in taking his eyes off her.

Justin had decided on a Roman costume, while his young cousin Harry was, as he laughingly said, a knight in cardboard armour.

"But dashed if I'm going to clank around in chain mail!" he declared in response to the gibes of his companions. "This fishnet stuff does the trick, don't it? Reckon I look the dandy, and you're all jealous!"

"I take it you're not dressing up, George?" demanded Justin, with a grin at his brother-in-law.

"Good God, no! Leave that sort of nonsense to you younger men," retorted Sir George. "A mask and a domino is my sole concession to the evening's frivolity."

It was his lady's, too, though she had been sorely tempted, at first, to go in historic costume, and several had actually been sent for her along with the others. But after having plagued her husband for several hours on the subject, she had decided against it, especially as nothing would induce him to go in fancy dress. The others were very well aware of this, and exchanged quizzical glances at Justin's sly remark.

3

MRS DE RYDE watched critically in the mirror as the maid completed a skilful arrangement of her coiffure which hid the grey hairs.

She nodded approvingly.

"Yes, well done, Healey. And now the gown."

She rose from the dressing table and prepared to step into an elegant gown of maroon silk, ruched and padded at the hem. The fastenings finished, she inspected herself before the long pier glass.

She was satisfied by the reflected image. Truly, her maid Healey was such a comfort. Over the years, she had dressed her mistress to the best advantage, concealing the tell-tale tricks of time. And it was quite a long time, thought Mrs de Ryde vaguely, her mind pre-occupied with her appearance, since her marriage twenty five years ago, when Healey had been very little older than herself, and she had been a bride of twenty summers.

"I think I'll wear *the necklace*, Healey," she announced.

The maid gasped.

"Madam, you'll never! After all we've heard lately of robberies, and — and — " her voice trailed off — "after what happened all those years agone, I think it's bad luck, that I do!"

"Nonsense," replied Mrs de Ryde, briskly. "We've been told that a Bow Street Runner will be in attendance. As for that bygone affair, why I've worn the necklace several times since then, and so you know. It would be foolish if I did not. The thief was apprehended and punished, so we need think no more of that. Come, I am waiting."

"Yes, ma'am."

Healey knew that she could presume so far and no farther. She produced a key from a tiny concealed drawer in the centre of the dressing table, and crossed to a mahogany inlaid cabinet against the window wall. She unlocked the cabinet, opened a small, velvet lined drawer, and produced a brilliant necklace of diamonds and rubies in an ugly old-fashioned setting.

She fastened this almost reverently around her mistress's neck.

Mrs de Ryde pursed her lips.

"It is not really to my taste — too heavy and clumsy. It doesn't show my neck to advantage."

This was true enough, for time had deprived her of that once smooth, girlish skin, and instead provided a set of creases and wrinkles and an incipient double chin. She sighed, raising her head to minimise the effect.

"Ah, well, one cannot expect an heirloom to look as well as a modish piece of jewellery. And it *is* prodigiously valuable, so that every female there will be envying me for possessing it."

She turned away from the mirror, demanding her domino mask, gloves, fan and reticule. Healey promptly supplied these, deftly adjusted the silk domino and buttoned the gloves. Then she ushered her mistress out of the room to descend the wide staircase and join her husband, Philip de Ryde, who was awaiting her with controlled impatience in the hall, a dark blue domino over his arm.

Presently they left the house to enter their carriage, on their way to the Assembly Rooms in York for the Lord Mayor's masquerade.

When they had gone, Healey busied herself with tidying up the dressing room after her mistress. She had almost completed her task when a knock came on the door. Knowing it would be one of the other servants, she opened it without any hesitation, a pair of her mistress's shoes still in her other hand.

One of the kitchen-maids stood outside, clutching a letter and looking sheepish.

"What are you doing here?" demanded Healey sharply, setting the shoes down behind the door.

The girl's confusion mounted. She held out the note.

"Please, m', t'lad who brought this to t'kitchen door said for me to give it thee mysen, not to pass it on to t'ousemaids or owt like that, please, m'. So I come upstairs knowin' as tha'd be 'ere, m', though to tell t'truth, I'm frit to death I'll be in 'ot water for it."

She looked uneasily about her.

"Well, give me the note, then clodpole!" snapped Healey. "And then you can take yourself off downstairs again. Wait — is the lad you mentioned still there? I've a mind to see him — I'll come with you."

The girl shook her head.

"Nay, m', he scarpered onct I'd sworn to tak' t'note to thee mysen. Made me swear on me Bible oath, 'e did — but 'e gi'ed me tuppence for me trouble."

Healey snorted, turning the piece of paper over in her fingers. It was directed to her in capital letters in a passable hand. Avid with curiosity as she was, she had no intention of opening it in front of the maid. She dismissed her sharply, then closed the door and opened the brief note.

She gasped and turned pale as she read its contents. She scanned it a second time, then a third, collapsing on to a chair as she did so.

"Oh, my Gawd!"

London born, she reverted to her Cockney accent only in times of great stress, otherwise her voice was schooled to the gentility of an upper servant.

She repeated the imprecation several times before rising unsteadily to her feet to glance at the ormolu clock on the mantelshelf.

It was close on nine o'clock. At this hour, most of the staff would be gathered in the servants' hall, with the master and mistress out of the way. If she slipped down the back staircase and used the side door, she ought to be safe enough from meeting anyone.

Ten minutes later, she was out in the grounds and heading for the ornamental temple beside the lake. The shadows were lengthening, and the August night was chilly. She shivered, pulling her cloak around her.

She mounted the steps to the pillared entrance of the temple with halting feet. It was dark inside the small, circular room, which was surrounded by a marble seat. She stood still, peering into the gloom.

A figure moved out of the shadows. She gave a loud gasp, starting back.

"Quiet!"

The voice was strange to her, yet it had a bygone familiar ring which at first she could not place.

"No harm will come to you — yet," the voice went on, in sinister tones. "That's if you're sensible, and do what I ask."

"Who are you — what d'ye want with me?" she panted. "How d'ye know about that business years agone — for Gawd's sake, leave me be!"

The unknown moved a pace nearer and took her arm in a firm but gentle grasp.

"No need for hysterics. Keep calm and listen."

In the gloom, she could just make out the glitter of eyes beneath a mask, and a cloaked male figure of medium height.

She gulped, trying to wrench her arm free. It was no use; his grip tightened until she winced with the pain.

"You'll come to no harm if you'll keep quiet and attend to me. Stand still."

Her struggles subsided, and he released her arm.

"Answer me this question," he ordered, brusquely. "Your mistress's brother — he still lives?"

"Sir Eustace Knowle?" Her tone was

surprised. "Ay — yes, that's to say — what of it?"

"By rights, he shouldn't," the man replied, grimly. "No matter. Where is he? Is he staying here?"

She shook her head. "No. Hasn't been here for more'n a twelvemonth."

The man gave a mirthless laugh. "He must have come into a mort of blunt, then. He always came to that stupid bitch of a sister when it was low water with him, and she never failed to haul him out of the river Tick." He stopped abruptly. "Where is he now? Tell me at once!"

"I don't know — how should I — "

She broke off as he seized her, shaking her like a dog with a rat.

"None o'that! You must know — you hear talk of him between Mr and Mrs de Ryde — he writes letters to your mistress, and I don't doubt she ain't the only one who reads 'em, what? Come on — out with it!"

"No, please! Honest to Gawd, I don't know — I swear it on my Bible oath — please believe me!"

"What do you know of the Bible, I

wonder?" he sneered, but he released her. "Very well, I believe you, woman. So you can find him out for me, understand? And you haven't got long — say two, three days from now — "

"But how?" She wrung her hands, on the verge of tears.

"You've a tongue in your head, I don't doubt, madam? Use it. If that don't answer, why, pry into her writing desk — won't be the first time. You'll find a way. You'd better, or else — "

"Yes, yes, I'll try, but how shall I let you know? That's if I do manage to find out — yes, I will, I will! For Gawd's sake, don't split on me — though how you know about that — "

She broke off with a gasp, as the underlying familiarity of his voice broke through to her.

"Oh, dear Gawd, you're not — !"

He nodded. She could not see his grim smile, but she sensed it.

"The same. So now you will know that I'm not to be trifled with. You'll find out this information for me, and you'll be useful to me in many other ways, too, I promise you. You will meet me here in three days' time — mark that well, Healey — at this same hour. If I am not here by half after nine, you will write the man Knowle's direction on a piece of paper, and hide it here."

He produced a dark lantern, sliding back one shutter a fraction so that a gleam of light fell across the floor.

"Over here!"

He seized her arm, thrusting her towards the marble bench which encircled the walls. Stooping, he directed the light underneath the bench to a tile in the floor. It was loose and yielded easily to the leverage of his fingers.

"Place the paper under here and press the tile well down again on top of it," he directed. "Not that anyone's likely to go groping about under this seat, I reckon."

He rose, closing the shutter so that the lantern's thin gleam was extinguished. The resultant gloom seemed deeper, more full of menace than before. Healey's teeth were chattering.

"Understand me?"

She nodded vigorously, unable to speak. He must have seen the movement, for he appeared satisfied.

"Good. And I needn't tell you to keep your mummer — " he relapsed into the vernacular — "shut. One word to anyone else — only a hint — and I'll make you wish you'd cut your tongue out first! Oh, yes, I promise you it don't pay to tip me the double, woman! Very well, begone!"

She believed him, and fled.

* * *

York's impressive Assembly Rooms had been designed by Lord Burlington in 1730 in the style of an Egyptian hall, colonnaded by Corinthian pillars with reddish brown marbling and capitals picked out in green, purple and gold. Normally, they were a blaze of light from several magnificent crystal chandeliers; but this evening only one had been lit, so that the great hall was dim enough to sustain the atmosphere of mystery essential to a masquerade.

"Upon my word," said Anthea, entering upon Justin's arm, "I doubt I need have taken so much trouble with my costume, for no one will be able to see it in this poor light."

"Sufficiently to suppose you the very reincarnation of Egypt's beauteous Queen, Miss Anthea," returned Rogers quickly, at her elbow. "Especially in this setting."

She turned to dimple at him, an effect unfortunately partly concealed by her mask.

"H'm," commented Justin, cynically, "Well, the lights will go up when the time comes for unmasking with the Lord Mayor's advent, just before supper. Until then, we may perhaps amuse ourselves in trying to guess the real identities of our fellow guests — those that are in costume, that is. It may prove an unprofitable exercise," he added, "since we're not acquainted with many people in York."

"No, it is not as easy as attending balls in London, where one is sure to know almost everyone," agreed Anthea. "But Aunt Julia can help — where is Aunt Julia, Louisa?"

"Uncle George has taken her to find one of the seats around the ballroom, before they become too crowded," replied

Louisa. "She bade me tell you that we must join her presently."

Anthea made no reply to this, as she was busy peering around her.

"That is Mr and Mrs de Ryde over there," she declared, after a moment. "But I claim no particular quickness in identifying them, since they aren't in costume! But the troubadour standing beside them — is he not, Louisa, that gentlemen who was paying you such particular attentions at the wedding — Mr — Mr — "

"Mr Giles Crispin," supplied Louisa, with a blush.

Anthea gave her a teasing look. "He has evidently solved the mystery of *your* identity, my dear. Look, he is coming this way."

By now it was well after the hour stated for the commencement of the ball, and the Master of Ceremonies decided that it was high time to begin the dancing. He directed his assistants to form the guests into sets for a cotillion, sweeping them on to the floor willy-nilly. As he pointed out, the true purpose of a masked ball was for all to mingle; and those who had no desire for this might sit out on the sofas and chairs provided behind the colonnade.

Those of the older guests who had not already done so, availed themselves of this facility; the rest went merrily into the dance, determined to enjoy themselves.

"I do trust," remarked his wife, as Sir George left her in a comfortable chair and prepared to take part in the revels, "that this won't develop into that kind of unseemly romp which one often used to see at Vauxhall. To dance with people whom one does not know — "

"Pooh, my dear, they're all here at the Lord Mayor's invitation and therefore quite unexceptionable," replied Sir George, as he made his way to the floor to join a set with a very attractive milkmaid as one of its members.

The cotillion concluded, another progressive country dance was begun. By now, there was a pleasant buzz of conversation and low laughter competing with the efforts of the musicians.

Suddenly, there was a faint scream from one of the ladies seated at the side of the room and signs of a disturbance in that quarter. Several couples ceased dancing to look that way; but in the dim light only those nearest could see what was happening. Among these were Anthea and Justin, whom the movements of the dance had for the moment brought together.

"B'Gad, it's an arrest!" exclaimed Justin, staring. "And none other than Joe Watts handing the culprit over to a constable — so *he* was the Bow Street Runner in attendance mentioned on our invitation card! Now, I wonder what's toward?"

By now everyone had stopped dancing and the Master of Ceremonies took the centre of the floor. He gave orders for the remaining chandeliers to be lit.

"No cause for alarm, ladies and gentlemen," he soothed. "The Bow Street Runner has everything under control — an attempt was made to pick a gentleman's pocket, but luckily Mr Watts was too sharp for the miscreant, and he's now on his way to the gaol. Pray resume the dance, ladies and gentlemen! You may rest quite secure under the watchful eye of our man from Bow Street.

It was an isolated instance which certainly will not occur again, I assure you most positively! Pray do continue!"

Most obeyed his plea, but one or two dropped out of the set. Justin was one. He made straight for Joseph Watts, who was in conversation with several of the town councillors.

Watts raised an eyebrow, but Justin signalled to him to finish his conversation, standing back a little while he did so.

"You here, guv'nor?" said Watts, when they were alone. "What brings you — some o' those ancient ruins o' yours?"

"This time the ancient ruin was my niece Marianne," grinned Justin. "But I'll allow that I'm staying on after her wedding in order to browse among the local antiquities. And you? I collect you were sent by Bow Street to guarantee the safety of the gee-gaws worn by guests tonight, since honourable mention is made of such a precaution on our invitation cards. What happened just now?"

"A prig at his game, sir. Luckily, I chanced to be moving his way in my rounds, and spotted him. Powerful quick, they are, too, the real pro's — prodigious sleight of hand! Though how he got in is another thing, seeing as there's a pair of constables on the door who should have known his phiz, being local men. Togged out like a footman, he was, and with so many on 'em, serving 'ere, who's to notice one brushing against you? Especially in that poor light. Did me a good turn, though, sir, for the aldermen here just asked me to stay on in York a while, keep my eyes open at the Races."

Justin nodded. "Plenty to do there, I dare say, though not much in our line, what? Still, I'm putting up at my brother-in-law's place at Firsdale — Sir George Marton, y'know — should you wish to call on my assistance," he added, with an ironical look.

Watts winked. "Never know, do ye, sir?"

The incident was soon forgotten and the dancing resumed. Anthea's costume was much admired and she found herself besieged by gentlemen eager to lead her into the set. It was almost time for the Lord Mayor's arrival before Sidney Rogers, after several unsuccessful applications, succeeded in partnering her.

"The Queen of Egypt at last deigns to honour a humble English cavalier," he said, as he took her hand. "I had quite abandoned hope, and was prepared to rush away and jump into the Fosse."

"What utter nonsense you do talk, sir!" All the same, her hazel eyes twinkled at him. "Humble, indeed! You are wearing a vastly rich costume!"

"Ah, but the fellow inside it feels humble enough," he assured her, solemnly. "Indeed, my pretensions are seriously depressed — I had hoped that my long acquaintance with Justin might predispose you to grant me a dance before this. But I see that I presumed too much." He sighed heavily.

She laughed; but as their hands touched in the movements of the dance, she felt a sudden and totally unexpected frisson of excitement. It caused her to sound severe when she answered him.

"Why do gentlemen always imagine that a girl wishes to be talked to in that extravagant style?" she scolded. "I declare, I've heard enough fulsome compliments for one evening. Surely you can address me in a more rational manner?"

He bowed with mock humility. "Your command is my law, ma'am. My only aim is to please you."

"Then pray don't flatter me," she recommended, suddenly serious. "It pleases me better for you to be yourself."

He grimaced. "You can have no notion how boring that would be."

"Truly? But why not try me?"

With a provocative glance she moved away from him into the set.

They were separated for a little while, and she found herself wondering what she really thought of him. She was used to attracting admirers wherever she went, and in general, enjoyed flirting harmlessly with them. She did not enjoy flirting nearly so much with Mr Rogers. Why? Not because she found him in any way repulsive or offensive to her sensibilities; on the contrary, she acknowledged that he was an undeniably attractive gentleman with practised address and a winning smile.

That was the trouble, she decided suddenly. Any of her other admirers could have been led on to pay serious addresses to her, had she wished this. Laughing, she held them off; and they accepted their fate resignedly, content to flirt with her until such time as she decided upon one or another.

But she was by no means certain that Mr Rogers meant anything at all by his flippant attentions.

How dare he trifle with her? It would be all the same, she thought indignantly and quite irrationally, if he had succeeded in making her fall in love with him. What a pretty pickle *that* would be! Fortunately, it was no such thing. She thought of what Justin had said about his friend having a mind of his own; and wondered if he, too, had noticed Aunt Julia's efforts to throw them together, and had decided to be on his guard. It was not a flattering reflection.

But Anthea could not long be serious, so she dismissed the matter from her mind; and when they were reunited in the set, she met him with a dazzling smile and a saucy glance.

The dance over, she returned to her aunt's side to find that lady deep in conversation with Mrs Cholmondley, a neighbour who had been present at the wedding. Mrs Cholmondley was complaining about her husband's habit of filling the house with people for Races Week.

"I declare I don't even know the half of them," she said. "And as the majority are men, there was never anything so boring! Oh, hush, here he comes with some of them — I do trust he'll present them to you himself, for I cannot be at all sure what their names are."

Anthea looked hastily about her for a way of escape, but failed to find one in time. She was obliged to remain while Mr Cholmondley, a plump gentleman with a genial countenance and manner, began to present his three companions to Aunt Julia and herself.

"But I protest, sir," put in Anthea, "it's not yet time for presentations! The company surely should remain anonymous until the Lord Mayor arrives and we all unmask?"

"Pooh, my dear Miss Rutherford, he'll be here at any moment! Besides, these gentlemen have been urging me for the past hour to present them to the prettiest young lady in the room!"

"In spite of my mask?" she retorted, saucily. "Thank you, gentlemen, for such a compliment!"

Sir John Fulford, Mr Fellowes and Mr Barnet were named to her and made their bows. Mr Fellowes looked ridiculous in a Tudor doublet and hose which made the worst of an ungainly paunch and bandy legs. Mr Barnet achieved a more creditable appearance in a Robin Hood costume, as he was taller, spare and had a complexion which suggested outdoor pursuits. Sir John Fulford, who was younger than his companions, was not in costume. He ogled her shamelessly; she tilted her chin.

"I owe a deal to Barnet here, 'pon my soul!" exclaimed Cholmondley. "Only the other day, he saved me from having my pocket picked, right in the middle of Micklegate, would you credit that?"

The two elder ladies exclaimed in

horror. Anthea looked curiously at Mr Barnet. He spread out his hands in a deprecating gesture.

"Happened to be passing," he said.

"And a good thing for me that you were so quick!" continued Cholmondley. "A great pity that the villain got away — but you were fully occupied in assisting me to my feet after I'd tripped up, and no one else was taking a confounded bit of notice! I don't know what we're coming to in York, 'pon my soul — even here, at the Lord Mayor's ball, one of those light-fingered gentry gains admittance!"

Lady Marton and Mrs Cholmondley agreed that it was monstrous. Anthea sighed, and looked across the room to where Justin was standing. Interpreting her signal of distress, he came over to the group. He was duly presented to Cholmondley's guests, but soon whisked her away.

"Thank goodness!" she exclaimed gratefully. "I do think the Cholmondleys of all people manage to assemble the most boring visitors, don't you? But tell me, Justin, how did you get on with Runner

Watts? Did you hear anything of interest from him?"

He shook his head. "No, a simple matter of a pickpocket loose in the Rooms, now on his way to the gaol."

She looked disappointed.

"Oh, well, I can quite see *that* won't be the start of one of our famous adventures!"

He laughed. "Just as well, madam. There were times during the last affair . . . however, no more of that! This is just a commonplace felony."

In the event, matters turned out to be far from commonplace.

4

THE gaming house in King Street, Covent Garden, was far from being one of London's most exclusive clubs, but it had resolutely closed its doors upon Sir Eustace Knowle. That gentleman was known to them of old as being not only a bit of a sharpster — which might be tolerated provided no one set up a squawk — but also as never having a feather to fly with, which was more serious from the management's point of view.

Eustace Knowle swore volubly, but there seemed nothing for it but to return to the sleazy lodging in Endell Street, which he had been obliged to make his quarters since returning from the Continent.

It had seemed such a good notion to visit Paris after the peace following Waterloo. At a time when there was bound to be confusion and disarray until everything settled down, surely an enterprising man could find pickings? It had proved to be just as difficult over there as here. The trouble was, he reflected ruefully, his tastes were damned expensive, and had always outrun his means, even when the old man had been alive and making him a reasonable allowance. But on the death of his father, Sir Ralph Knowle, there had been an abrupt end to this; thanks to his only son's extravagance, nothing had been left but debts and a heavily mortgaged, neglected property. Eustace Knowle had promptly disposed of this, and had been unsuccessfully attempting to live on the proceeds ever since.

He let himself into the dim hallway, almost falling over the cat as he entered. The animal gave a dismal mew and shot out into the night. At the same moment, a sharp faced individual in shirt sleeves emerged from the rear premises.

"Oh, it's you," he said, with a marked lack of enthusiasm.

"Bring in a bottle," commanded Knowle in slightly slurred accents, not deigning to respond to this greeting.

"Bottle, is it?" snorted the other. "Not

without I sees yer blunt, guv'nor."

"Here, damn you!" Knowle tossed a coin on the floor with a fine air of abandon. "That's more than it's worth, too — hogwash!"

The man picked up the coin, bit it ostentatiously, then put it into his pocket.

He shuffled off, and Knowle flung open the door of his sanctum, and lit the candle.

A dreary room was revealed, with very little furniture, and that of poor quality. A bed huddled in one corner; near a small, grimy window stood a table and chairs, and against one wall a hanging cupboard with drawers beneath.

The landlord, for such he was, pushed his way into the room without troubling to knock, and deposited a bottle of dubious wine and a thick glass upon the table. Without another word on either side, he went out, closing the door vigorously.

Knowle extracted the cork from the bottle and poured himself a glass. He grimaced as he took the first few gulps.

"Pah!"

He banged the glass down on the table, crossed over to the cupboard and pulled open a drawer. A litter of papers spilled out onto the floor.

He groaned. "Bills — nothing but damned bills! Hell and the devil, I'll have to clear out! But where?"

Not for the first time, he passed all his relatives and acquaintances in rapid mental review. Too many of them had indicated on the last occasion of a visit from him that they preferred his room to his company. Not that he was particularly sensitive to hints; but he did prefer a pleasant atmosphere, and there was no escaping the fact that some of his unwilling hosts had turned positively hostile.

There was, of course, his sister Mary. He hesitated. Mary was easy; she would give him anything he asked. On the other hand, her husband Philip . . .

His mouth twisted wryly. Philip had made no secret of the fact that his wife's brother was not at all welcome in his house. Ever since that clumsy business years since, reflected Eustace, what little credit he had ever possessed with Philip de Ryde had disappeared never to return. His few visits there of late years had been brief and undertaken only in circumstances of the direst necessity, because de Ryde made himself so damned unpleasant.

He shrugged. The present crisis was one of those times. His sister's house was the only refuge remaining to him until something or other turned up to his advantage. He was an incurable optimist, never doubting that his luck would change. It occurred to him suddenly, thinking of luck, that this was the month of the York Races. Perhaps fortune might favour a flutter on the nags — provided he could raise the wind, of course. He smiled as he reflected that Mary would find the ready. She quite doted on him, good old Mary.

He bent over to stuff the bills back into the drawer, slamming it shut with one foot. He considered his negotiable assets for a moment. It did not take long, for most of these were already reposing in the pawnbroker's shop. He pulled from his pocket a gold snuff box set with precious stones, and tipped the contents on to a piece of paper that he had failed to thrust back into the drawer.

He nodded, satisfied. The proceeds from that article would pay his fare to York.

* * *

On the morning after the masquerade, Mr and Mrs de Ryde were late appearing at the breakfast table. Their daughter Anne and the governess, Miss Fawcett, had been staying overnight with the Martons and had not yet returned home, so there were only the two of them.

"I declare," said Mrs de Ryde, stifling a yawn, "one almost feels that it's not worth the pleasure of a ball, for the fatigue one suffers the next day! And it was not such a pleasurable affair, after all. I found most of the company insipid."

"Good God!" exclaimed her husband, suddenly.

She stared. "I'm sure I see no reason why you should be so surprised, my dear. They are, after all, most of them people we've known for ever."

"What?" He raised his eyes abstractedly from the letter in his hand, for he had been opening his post. "Oh, it's not anything you've said — I've just opened the most extraordinary letter — a damnable letter, in fact!"

"Oh, dear," she replied, in tones of dismay. "What is it, Philip? Who has sent it?"

"That I can't tell you, but this I do know, the fellow's a madman!"

He jumped to his feet, screwing the letter into a ball and tossing it contemptuously into the fireplace.

"Can't tell me? But surely there's a signature?" she demanded, puzzled.

"No such thing. And if I'd written that rubbish, I wouldn't have put my name to it, either, I can tell you!"

"Can you mean — can you possibly mean — that it's an *anonymous* letter, Philip?"

He nodded. "Not only that, but threatening, too. Come to think of it — " he strode across to retrieve the paper from the fireplace, frowning heavily — "perhaps I ought to show it to George Marton."

"Show it to Sir George? But why in the world — oh, I see!" she exclaimed all at once, in tones of enlightenment. "You mean, because he's a Justice of the Peace? You want to lay an information against this — this unknown person? Well, if it's a threatening letter, I should think you're very wise. But who would threaten you — and why? Let me see it."

He shook his head and stuffed the letter into his pocket.

"And have you fretting yourself into a distemper over some lunatic's maunderings? No, my love, I know well your capacity for making a mountain out of a molehill!"

Returning to the table, he bent over and lightly kissed his wife's cheek. She patted her hair complacently; it was something to have one's husband paying one small attentions after five and twenty years. No doubt he was right about that stupid letter. There were always enough things to vex her without going out of her way to find them.

Anne returned with her governess just as breakfast was over and Mrs de Ryde was wondering how she should spend the morning. Her husband had retired to the library.

Anne came bursting into the morning room, full of energy, making her mother feel even more fatigued.

She planted a dutiful morning peck on her mama's cheek, and burst into exuberant voice.

"Oh, Mama, did you enjoy the masquerade yesterday evening? Fanny's cousins, Miss Rutherford and Miss Harvey, say it was famous fun, and — and Mr Harvey — " she blushed on saying the name, for nineteen year old Henry Harvey was at present the subject of her schoolgirl fancy — "said it was not at all bad. Of course, he would not enthuse, you know, for gentlemen rarely do, do they? But he did tell me that something occurred to stir them all up a bit, as he put it. Fancy, Mama, a *pickpocket* loose in the Assembly Rooms! And at the Lord Mayor's ball, too! But Mr Harvey says that the man was very soon arrested by a Bow Street Runner who was keeping watch there. Mama, I do so wish I'd been present! Not only for *that*, of course, but so that I might have seen all the costumes, and guessed who their wearers might be! Mama, do you think I'll be able to attend the ball next year? I shall be seventeen, and then, and — "

"Oh, my dear child, pray stop!" implored Mrs de Ryde, putting her hands to her head. "I've the most frightful headache, and your rattling on makes it worse!"

Anne looked contrite, for she was a well meaning girl.

"I'm sorry, Mama. Perhaps Papa will tell me all about it — is he in the library?"

"Yes, but I don't think you'd better disturb him at present," replied her mother, hastily. "He's somewhat put out this morning."

"Put out? Why?" Anne was incurably curious.

"Oh, I don't know. Some letter he received."

"Letter? Who from, Mama?"

"From whom?" corrected Mrs de Ryde, automatically.

"Oh, very well, from whom?" agreed

Anne, in an impatient tone.

There was silence for a moment.

"Well, don't you mean to tell me?" insisted the girl.

Her mother sighed. "I can't, for I don't know. Now, pray, Anne, run up to the schoolroom, and don't pester me. I am most odiously fatigued this morning, there was never anything like it! Oh, and on your way, look in at my boudoir and desire Healey to bring me my vinaigrette."

Seeing there was nothing more to be gleaned from her mother, Anne obediently departed. She was familiar with mama's strategic headaches, and wondered on her way upstairs just what this letter could be that had upset Papa, usually an imperturbable man. She decided that most likely Mama was exaggerating, as she obviously felt somewhat out of sorts this morning.

She pushed open the door of her mother's boudoir without ceremony. Then she stopped short and stared.

Mrs de Ryde's elegant little writing bureau stood against the opposite wall of the small room. The top was open, and Healey was in the act of hunting desperately through the pigeon holes when Anne came into the room.

The maid started violently, dropping a piece of paper on the floor. She put a hand to her heart.

"Oh, miss, you frightened me!"

"I can see that," replied Anne, unsympathetically. "Just what are you about in my mother's bureau, Healey?"

"Oh — oh — Madam asked me to look for — for a bill from the milliner's," gasped the maid, desperately, "to see if it had been paid."

"And when did she ask you to do this?" demanded Anne, coldly.

"When I was dressing her, Miss Anne." Healey did her best to control the tremor in her voice. "Only — only I didn't think of it until now."

"Indeed. Well, she wants you to take her vinaigrette to the morning room. She has the headache."

Anne crossed to the bureau, picked up the dropped piece of paper from the floor and scrutinised it. She saw it was a letter from her grandmother.

She restored it to one of the pigeon

holes and closed the lid of the bureau firmly.

"At once," she ordered, as she left the room.

She frowned as she turned towards the schoolroom. She did not believe a word of Healey's excuse. What had the maid really been doing? And why were letters so prominent a feature in this morning's events?

* * *

An inclination to lethargy likewise afflicted the Marton household that morning. Only Justin and his friend Sidney Rogers appeared to have survived the previous evening's dissipation without the necessity for a lie-in. Justin, his dark curly hair brushed into some semblance of order at this early hour of the day, strode into the breakfast parlour with a firm, decisive step. Rogers, who had just lifted the cover from a dish of kidneys on the sideboard, looked up momentarily to give him good morning.

"Don't interrupt a chap when he's engaged on matters of importance," he added, returning to his task of selection.

Justin seized a plate and likewise passed the dishes in review.

"And what have you in mind to do this morning?" asked Rogers, when he had returned with a heaped-up plate to the table.

"Visit Sheriff Hutton," replied Justin, joining him.

Rogers raised his brows. "Who? I was thinking I might accompany you, but if you're seeing some old curmudgeon — "

Justin laughed. "Not who — what," he corrected.

"Mm? 'Fraid I don't follow you."

"Sheriff Hutton's a place. A ruined castle, to be precise, not far from here. I've a fancy to see it."

His brown eyes glinted with enthusiasm, an expression his friend knew well.

"It goes back to the twelfth century and played an important part in the Wars of the Roses, but it became neglected in the early seventeenth century, and parts of it were dismantled to provide the stone for other local buildings."

"So its ruined state wasn't due to that old despoiler of castles, Cromwell?" asked

Rogers, who had an interest himself in historical subjects.

"Not this time. Well, d'you think you'll come?"

Rogers assented, and, disposing of the meal quickly, they made their way to the stables.

They were surprised to find their host there before them. He was about to mount his bay Rowley — an animal that had drawn forth the other men's favourable comments when first Sir George had shown them round the stables on their arrival at Firsdale Hall. They exchanged greetings.

"We're off to take a look at the ruined castle at Sheriff Hutton, George," explained Justin, while two of the grooms led out their horses.

Sir George swung himself into the saddle.

"Capital," he approved. "That should keep you busy until dinner time, if I know you, Justin. Don't let him bore you to death, Rogers."

"No fear of that," laughed Rogers. "I'm quite partial to antiquities, myself."

"Well, amuse yourselves. I'm off on

business, worse luck — over to Thwaite's farm, see one of my tenants. Opposite way from you."

He nodded, then paused as he was about to move off, frowning at one of the grooms.

"You're new, ain't you? Don't recollect your face."

The man touched his cap.

"Yes, sir."

"We took on an extra couple of hands for the wedding, Sir George," explained the other man, who had been head groom at Firsdale Hall for many years. "This is Leckby, and t'other's Ross. He's in t'tackroom. Was you wishful to see him, sir?"

"No, no. Very good, Carr."

With a dismissive nod and a wave of his hand to his guests, he rode away. The farm where he was bound was only three or four miles distant, so he rode easily, letting his horse set the pace at first. His way led through narrow, twisting lanes skirting the edges of fields high with golden corn soon to be harvested. Presently, he reached a meadow where sheep grazed. He turned off the lane here, along a little used bridleway running between the hedge and a stretch of dense woodland on his right. It was a bumpy ride over rough, uneven ground; but he cared little for that, as it offered a short cut to his objective.

Suddenly, a shot sounded from the trees close beside him and he felt a sharp sting as a bullet grazed his cheek. Startled, he loosed his hold on the rein for a moment. The horse, too, was startled; it reared in protest, and threw him heavily to the ground.

"What the devil?" he shouted. "Here, stand still, Rowley, damn you!" The horse obeyed instantly.

Sir George attempted to rise to his feet, but found to his chagrin that this was far from easy. His right ankle had been twisted under him in the fall, and now it was extremely painful to put it to the ground. His first thought had been to chase into the wood after the person who had fired the shot, but now this proved impossible. With difficulty, he raised himself up, standing upon one leg, and shouted to the hidden, and no doubt mistaken, marksman to come forth and explain himself.

His challenge was greeted by a profound silence. Then in the distance he heard the sound of a horse's hoofs retreating through the wood.

He cursed long and volubly, as a trickle of blood from his wound made its way into his mouth and down his neck. He wiped it angrily away with a handkerchief, then looked about him for a means of mounting his horse again. He soon espied a log not many yards away at the side of the track, and, gritting his teeth, set himself to the task of making his way to it. His horse, a well trained animal in rapport with its master, seemed to understand what was wanted of it, and placed itself strategically beside the log in readiness.

The business of mounting on its back was both painful and time consuming. Meanwhile, blood flowed freely from the grazed cheek unhindered, for all Sir George's energies were concentrated on the main task. At last he was up in the saddle, however, and able to continue on his way, with one foot dangling.

His arrival at Thwaite's farm caused

quite a stir. The sight of Squire with blood all over his cravat and mud on his riding coat and breeches was not something to which they were accustomed. He would have no fuss, however, and it was with difficulty that Mrs Thwaite managed to persuade him to have the grazed cheek bathed and dressed.

"Though reckon doctor ought to take a look at it, Squire," she cautioned him, as she bore away the bowl of bloodied water. "Happen might turn nasty."

"Fustian — only a scratch," he persisted. "But I'll borrow your gig, Jack, if I may, and I'll send a groom over for the bay."

He frowned thoughtfully. "Know of anyone who'd have a sporting gun out in the wood?"

"No, Sir George. Fair puzzles me, that do. Barrin' poachers, an' mostly they comes after dark, can't think of anyone who'd go after rabbits or birds, not in t'wood. And there's nowt else."

"And I don't look much like either, wouldn't you say?" demanded Sir George, with a grim chuckle.

The farmer grinned. "Reckon not, Squire. But it fair flummoxes me, an' no mistake. I'll just be keepin' an eye on that wood in future."

Sir George grunted, but said no more.

The three girls, Anthea, Louisa and Fanny, were about to set out on a stroll to the village when Farmer Thwaite's gig came up the drive with Sir George seated inside.

"Why, Papa!" exclaimed Fanny, running up to the modest equipage and staring. "What in the world are you doing in Mr Thwaite's gig?"

"Mind your manners, chit," replied her father, curtly.

Thus reproved, Fanny greeted the farmer civilly, and he responded by touching his cap.

"But — but — Papa — there's blood on your neckcloth!" she gasped, alarmed.

"Never mind that, but just get one of the footmen to help me into the house," he said, shortly. "I've ricked my ankle."

But Anthea, who had realised at once that some accident had occurred to her uncle, had already summoned help. Two footmen attended by the butler, came quickly down the steps of the house and advanced upon the gig.

"No need to kick up a devilish fuss," Sir George directed Oldroyd, as he was helped into the house. "Don't want Lady Marton disturbed. Help me into the library and give me a glass of the madeira. I'll do very well — no need for you girls to come with me."

"But, Papa, what has happened?" demanded Fanny, shocked to the core.

"Not now — later," replied Sir George, tersely, hopping along with one hand on a sturdy footman's shoulder. "Don't bother me now, there's a good girl."

Feeling Anthea tugging at her skirt, Fanny subsided. Anthea turned to the farmer for information, and he quickly told them all he knew.

She listened with knitted brows.

"You say you don't know of anyone likely to have been out shooting in that wood?" she asked, at the end of his recital. "Is there another farm nearby?"

"Plenty in t'neighbourhood, ma'am, but not close to t'wood. I'm right sorry about Squire, an' it fair puzzles me 'ow he could come to be hit. Stands to reason they must've been after rooks or pigeons, I reckon, t'ave aimed so high, but wonder is, they didn't spot him, an' hold their fire." He shook his head. "Can't get to t'bottom o' it, at all. Well, Squire said to take up one o' t'grooms from t'stables to bring back his bay, so reckon I'd best be movin', ma'am."

The girls thanked him in unison, then decided to continue with their walk, although at first Fanny was reluctant to leave her father.

"If you have any thoughts of mopping his fevered brow and administering sal volatile," said Anthea, in a rallying but not unkind tone, "then I advise you to dismiss them, Fanny! Gentlemen dislike fuss in such cases — moreover, in general it makes them feel worse. Oldroyd will supply his needs adequately, I feel confident. And it wouldn't surprise me if my aunt, when she hears of it, as she's bound to do, sends for the doctor."

This prediction turned out to be accurate. When the girls returned to Firsdale Hall a few hours later, the Martons' medical man had been to visit Sir George. He confirmed that the bullet wound was merely a graze which would soon heal, but professed himself puzzled as to how the marksman came to inflict it.

"He must have seen you," he objected, "unless he loosed off a pot shot impulsively at a bird flying over your head."

"There were no birds flying anywhere near me," asserted Sir George, firmly.

"Then you must have an enemy, Sir George," returned the doctor, jocularly.

His patient gave an involuntary start. Quickly controlled though it was, the trained medical eye did not miss it. Dr Clent raised his brows.

"Do you?" he asked, bluntly.

"No such thing! Just some trigger-happy fool, and I chanced to be in his line of fire."

"H'm," said the doctor, non-committally. "Well, that ankle will need resting for a few weeks. It's not a bad sprain, as sprains go, but it will keep you off your feet for a while. Good day to you."

Sir George nodded absently. His thoughts were elsewhere.

5

IT was close on dinner time when Justin and Rogers returned to Firsdale Hall, well satisfied with their day's outing. Anthea, on her way upstairs, informed them briefly of the accident.

"Good God!" exclaimed Justin. "I take it the chap with the gun explained himself and apologised? Who was he — anyone old George knows?"

"No such thing," replied Anthea. "Uncle George never so much as set eyes on whoever did it. He says he heard a horse moving off in the distance, though. He couldn't go in pursuit, because of his sprained ankle."

"Well, I'm damned!"

Both men looked at each other in disgust.

"Fired in error, and then too chicken-hearted to own up?" suggested Rogers. "Slung his hook on the spur of the moment? Might be regretting it now, ready to come forward and apologise.

Devilish shabby, even so."

"It *could* be like that, of course," said Anthea slowly.

"Now, don't you go refining too much upon what is most likely an unfortunate mistake," Justin chided her. "If you're getting maggots in your head about an assassin wanting to kill George, forget it. Anyone intending murder wouldn't have been satisfied with a mere graze on the cheek, which is what you say it is."

"He might have missed," protested his niece.

"Reluctant to lose your drama?" scoffed Justin. "Nothing to stop him from taking a second shot, was there? Especially as poor old George was a sitting duck at that time."

"No, I suppose not," said Anthea, reluctantly. "Well, I must go upstairs to change for dinner."

Later, when the whole party was assembled round the table, talk of his accident was quickly squashed by Sir George. Instead, he steered the conversation into general topics. Once the ladies had left the dining room, it was a simple matter to avoid any mention of the incident in the very natural interest aroused by the forthcoming race meetings. The points of the various runners were animatedly debated, and his mishap forgotten, which was precisely as he wished.

* * *

The wedding of Sir George and Lady Marton's eldest daughter had taken place in York's beautiful Minster, but in general the family attended the local church of St Peter. It was an ancient building with a Norman arch over the west door and traces of mediaeval paintings remaining on the walls of the nave.

Fanny Marton and Anne de Ryde had been especially ready to attend service this morning, for they both wished to see the new curate. It was not that they were really interested in the clergy in general; but rumour — in the person of one of their other neighbours' young daughters — had it that the Reverend Bernard Kent was not only a bachelor in his mid twenties, but a personable gentleman into the bargain. This turned out to be true, and they had the felicity of being presented to him by the vicar after the services. They discussed his merits in confidential tones while their elders were chatting together in the churchyard, and agreed that his coming would lend a spice of interest to local life.

Lady Marton had already told her neighbours briefly about the unfortunate accident which had prevented her husband from attending the service that morning, but Anne's curiosity had not been so easily satisfied. She now insisted on hearing every particular from Fanny, on exclaiming over it and examining it as best she could for an explanation which satisfied her.

"Depend upon it, someone will present himself at the house in a day or so to apologise," she said, having exhausted the topic. "And that reminds me, Fanny, I have something very odd to tell you! When I reached home yesterday, I caught my mother's maid, Healey, prying into mama's bureau! Of course, she *said* she was looking for some bill or other on Mama's instructions, but I believe it was no such thing, for when I asked Mama later, she seemed not to recollect it. But then, Mama was not in a humour to attend much to what I said. She was fatigued after the ball, you know — after all, ladies of her age — " They both nodded sagely, from the security of their sixteen years — "and then Papa had just received a disturbing letter, and would not tell her what was in it."

"But Healey has been with your mother all of her married life, has she not?" asked Fanny, ready to enter into anything which intrigued her friend. "She wouldn't have any reason to pry — she must be familiar with all the details of Mrs de Ryde's concerns, as every old and trusted servant is. I am sure our butler Oldroyd, knows things about us that we ourselves have forgotten, for he's been in Papa's service for ever!"

"True," replied Anne, consideringly. "And that's what made me wonder . . . She looked so guilty when I surprised her. Now, what can she have been after?"

Speculation on this point was cut short, as the groups broke up and parents reclaimed their offspring to transport them home.

In the afternoon, however, Fanny persuaded Anthea to walk the short distance with her to her friend's home, Denby House, the adjoining property to Firsdale Hall. The walk occupied only a leisurely twenty minutes, but during this time Fanny insisted on acquainting her cousin with everything that had passed between Anne de Ryde and herself that morning. Anthea was very much amused by the artless chatter about the new curate. It reminded her of her own schooldays, which already, at only nineteen, seemed far in the past. Her easily aroused curiosity flickered for a moment over the story of Mrs de Ryde's maid, but soon died away for lack of any supporting information. After all, she thought with a shrug, old servants did take a few liberties now and then, but obviously were to be trusted in the main or they would never survive to become old servants.

Arriving at Denby House, they were shown into the drawing room where the family were sitting. There was a gentleman with them whom Anthea had not previously met. He came at once to his feet, and Anthea inspected him critically as Mr de Ryde presented him, somewhat austerely, as Anthea thought.

"Miss Rutherford, pray allow me to present Sir Eustace Knowle, my wife's brother. Eustace, Miss Rutherford is niece to Lady Marton. And you'll no doubt recall Miss Fanny Marton from your previous visits."

H'm, thought Anthea, as they shook hands and exchanged bows. Not bad looking for a man of about forty, though perhaps a trifle raddled; a vast deal of charm in that smile and, yes, undoubtedly he was eyeing her with full appreciation. She flashed one of her provocative smiles at him, always ready to offer harmless encouragement.

"And little Miss Fanny, of course," said Sir Eustace in genial tones, turning to the younger girl. "But Jove, how you've grown! No longer little — quite the young lady, I see."

Fanny blushed as she stammered a greeting.

"Uncle Eustace said just the same thing to me," put in Anne, jumping up to make room for Anthea on the sofa next to Mrs de Ryde. "As though one didn't change in more than a twelvemonth, which is the period since he last visited us! But I think he means it kindly, all the same."

"Can there be any doubt?" asked Sir Eustace, in tones of deep admiration. "Two such lovely young creatures — "

"Come, come, Eustace, that's doing it too brown," said de Ryde, testily.

"Yes, you'll be making them vain," agreed his wife, "and that will never do. Miss Fawcett is at vast pains to instil the principles of modesty into Anne, but I fear I cannot rate her success too highly."

Anthea said lightly that her governess, too, had found this uphill work; a remark which earned her a look of gratitude from the two girls, an amused grin from both the gentlemen, and a glance of cold disapproval from Mrs de Ryde.

Anthea knew very little of the lady, but Mrs de Ryde was not a female to inspire instant liking in the bosoms of her own sex. Indeed, Anthea wondered how it was that such a mother came to have an open, friendly daughter like Anne, and she credited it to Philip de Ryde's account. During the conversation that ensued, inevitably she and Mrs de Ryde talked together for the most part, as they were seated side by side. They chatted of the masquerade, of that morning's sermon, and finally of the latest fashions, Mrs de Ryde wishing Anthea to know that York was in no way inferior to London in the matter of modish dress. Anthea very soon became bored, and after the ritual tea drinking, signified to Fanny that it was time to depart.

Sir Eustace promptly offered to escort them home, and Anne seized upon this chance of prolonging her chat to Fanny by begging for permission to go with them, since Uncle Eustace would be there to accompany her back.

The four set out together. Soon the two girls were walking ahead of their elders, deep in conversation, leaving Sir Eustace and Anthea in peace to conduct what looked like being a very promising flirtation.

"I collect you live in London, Miss Rutherford? I'm frequently there myself — have a set of rooms, y'know. It's a thousand pities that we've never chanced to meet, but all the fashionable social gatherings are such frightful crushes, what?"

Anthea, who was nobody's fool, reflected that had this gentleman moved in her own social circle, they would have been bound to meet at some time or other. Still, he was a gentleman, charming, entertaining, and obviously prepared to admire her. What more could a girl ask on a dull Sunday afternoon in the country?

"Oh, well, as to that," she answered, with a shrug. "And I dare say you avoid Almack's like the plague — indeed, I don't go there very often myself, it is too odiously prosy."

He smiled admiringly down at her.

"Prosy, indeed. And yet I feel that wherever you go, ma'am, any man lucky enough to be in your vicinity must find the prosiest place transformed."

"Oh, sir!" she exclaimed, in simple milkmaid style. "You must recollect Mrs de Ryde's strictures on making females vain. Such flattery will surely go to my head!"

He laughed. "I doubt it, consummate

actress that you evidently are. But — " in a more serious tone — "you must permit me to tell you that you are a remarkably attractive young lady, Miss Rutherford, and that I hope to be allowed to pursue our acquaintance further."

She pretended to consider this, head on one side, looking up at him archly from beneath the brim of a delectable straw bonnet trimmed with pink ruched satin.

"Well, I don't see why not," she said, in her open, candid way. "I shall be staying with my aunt for the next few weeks, until my parents return from a visit to the Lakes, and I am quite sure she will be delighted to have you call on her."

"But it is not your *aunt* whom I wish to see, ma'am, as you must surely understand. Doubtless my sister will bring me to do the polite thing at Firsdale Hall — " he grimaced slightly, and she gave an understanding smile — "but can we not, say, go riding or driving together, you and I? Soon — tomorrow, perhaps?"

He halted momentarily, turning towards

her with an appealing outflung hand and a pleading expression on his face.

She laughed softly. "Indeed, sir, you go to work with prodigious speed! You quite outpace me, I do declare! We have but just met, recollect — how long since? All of sixty minutes!"

"Sixty minutes or sixty weeks — what can it signify, ma'am? What matters time in affairs of the heart?"

He will be quoting the poets next, thought Anthea, amused; but no, I cannot quite believe that he is a literary kind of man. She looked severe, and said aloud, "Pooh, Sir Eustace, you mustn't talk so! As for driving out with you tomorrow, I regret that I have a previous engagement. But the Races will be on for the remainder of the week, and I dare say I shall be at the Knavesmire some of the time with the rest of my family. Doubtless we shall see you there."

He said she was cruel and bemoaned his fate. For the rest of the way, the flirtation was conducted on classic lines, he flattering her and she playfully chiding. They were both expert, so did it well, enjoying themselves tolerably in the process.

This was evident to Justin and Rogers, who met the party on their way up the drive to the house.

"Who is that damned fellow with Miss Anthea?" demanded Rogers, *sotto voce*, as they approached.

Justin shook his head. "No notion, Sprog. Must be some relative of young Anne de Ryde's, I'd say. Getting on famously with Anthea, ain't he? Not a bad looking chap, either."

Rogers grunted an imprecation, and Justin looked amused.

⋆ ⋆ ⋆

When Sir Eustace Knowle had arrived at Denby House earlier that afternoon, only his sister Mary had been genuinely pleased to see him. Philip de Ryde knew from past experience that the fellow never turned up unless he was deep in the River Tick, and that Mary would be fool enough to tow him out, as usual. His appearance in their midst always led to quarrels between husband and wife.

As for Anne, a visit from her uncle was a matter of indifference. She cared no more for him than he did for her.

But to one person his appearance came as a dispensation of providence. Healey had been in a state of terror ever since her meeting two days since with the threatening figure in the temple by the lake. She had searched frantically through her mistress' correspondence in the desperate hope of finding some clue to Sir Eustace's whereabouts. She had found nothing; and now only one day remained before she must present herself at the rendezvous and admit failure. What the retribution would be was a living nightmare to the wretched woman. Her state had not gone unnoticed by her mistress, little though Mrs de Ryde was in the habit of observing such things among the servants. She had mentioned to her husband that perhaps it was time for her to part company with Healey.

"Though how I shall contrive to go on with a new abigail is more than I can conceive," she complained, bitterly. "Healey knows just how to dress me to advantage, and how long will it take another to learn her skills? Besides, we are used to each other, she and I. But I tell you, Philip, there's no bearing with her nerviness and absence of mind lately! And what right, I ask you, has a servant to suffer from nervous spasms — for that is what one would call it in a lady!"

Over the past few days, Healey had used her best endeavours to overhear every conversation between her employers; listening in successfully to this one did nothing to calm her state of panic.

When, therefore, Sir Eustace Knowle arrived unexpectedly at Denby House early on Sunday afternoon, she was hard put to it not to swoon outright on hearing the news from Oldroyd in the servants' hall. Cook looked appraisingly at her, then pushed her gently into a chair, recommending a good strong cup of tea. Healey accepted this panacea, afterwards retiring to her bedchamber to recover.

"Poor crittur," said Cook, compassionately, as the sufferer left the room. "But it's not to be wondered at — " lowering her voice to exclude the male section of the household staff — "when a female gets to be 'er age, there's queer starts, think on. I knows mysen, none better."

Which dark remark impressed every female present except the tweeny maid, who so far forgot herself as to giggle, thus earning a sharp reprimand.

By the time Healey came down again she was in command of herself, and knew just what she meant to do.

She was certainly not going to present herself at the temple in the grounds tomorrow evening, as her tormentor had commanded. No, she could not bear to face him again; moreover, there was now no need. She had only to write a note and leave it in the spot which he had indicated. She could easily find an opportunity later this evening to slip outdoors unnoticed.

She had a moment's misgiving when she recalled that he had spoken of employing her for other purposes, but she pushed the thought away. If he wanted to seek her out, he would find his own means of access, no doubt; but she very much hoped that he would be satisfied with the information that Sir Eustace was here in Denby House. She wondered uneasily where he was concealing himself, and shivered to think that he might be uncomfortably close at hand. What use he might make of Sir Eustace's presence here was another disturbing reflection. She shivered, doing her utmost to dismiss the terror that had possessed her for the past few days. She told herself that she no longer had anything to fear, for she was about to obey his instructions.

6

THE Knavesmire, site of York's Race meetings, was originally a marsh; but in 1730 the wardens of Micklegate were ordered to drain it, then level and roll the ground for horse racing. The first meeting took place there in the following year, and subsequently became an annual event. In the 1750's, a fine grandstand designed by the architect John Carr was erected to accommodate genteel racegoers; but, in common with other tracks throughout the country, the ground was always crammed with people from all walks of society. Elegant ladies walked about twirling their parasols or sat in carriages picnicking; their menfolk perched on the roof of the vehicles, or pushed their way to the paddock to watch the horses parading with their jockeys in a colourful spectacle. Persons of a more vulgar stamp mingled freely with the Quality, some there for love of the sport, others for more nefarious purposes. All manner of sideshows assembled nearby with vendors bellowing their wares: peep shows, pea and thimble tables, and even a fortune-teller's booth.

This latter attraction caught Anthea's eye when she arrived at the Knavesmire with the party from Firsdale Hall. She halted before it.

"I positively must see what the future has in store for me!" she exclaimed. "What say you, Louisa? Shall we venture in?"

"Do not be so absurd, Anthea!" snapped her Aunt Julia. "Surely even you couldn't be so outrageous as to enter such a — such a flea-bitten, unspeakable place! The notion quite appals me!"

"Which is what she wished it to do, dear Julia," said Justin, with a grin. "How you do rise to the bait, don't you?"

She was about to turn on him with an angry retort, but at that moment they were strolling past the de Rydes, who were accompanied by Sir Eustace Knowle. They halted to exchange greetings, and Sir Eustace soon managed to manoeuvre himself next to Anthea.

He had been observing her party for some little time before they exchanged greetings with his, and referred at once to the argument between Anthea and Lady Marton.

"Couldn't help overhearing," he said, with a disarming smile, "that there's something you wish to do that don't meet with your aunt's approval. Dare say it's not an infrequent dilemma — but pray satisfy my curiosity, impudent though you may think me for asking?"

Seeing no reason why she should not tell him, she did so, then joined in his laughter at the reply.

"Oh, famous!" he exclaimed. "And why not? Tell you what, Miss Anthea, if you can contrive to shake off your chaperone, I'll escort you into the booth."

She saw that Rogers was scowling at her while he was trying to maintain a polite conversation with Mrs de Ryde, Aunt Julia and Louisa. She tilted her chin defiantly.

"Truly?" she answered, with a roguish look. "Well, I'd certainly like to see Petula, Queen of the Gipsies, and hear what she may tell me — not that I believe in such stuff, I promise you, but it's tremendous fun!"

"To be sure, and where's the harm?" returned Sir Eustace. "See, there's a party of highly respectable gentlefolk about to enter now. Tell you what, ma'am, I'll hang about here until you turn up, be it never so long, I promise you!"

She laughed, but shook her head at him reproachfully.

Just then, they were approached by the Cholmondleys and a small group of their house guests, including the three who had accompanied them to the masquerade: Sir John Fulford, Mr Barnet and Mr Fellowes. The latter looked slightly less absurd in sporting attire than he had in Tudor costume. Mr Barnet appeared much the same; he favoured Anthea with a long stare, Justin observed. But it was Fulford who moved forward out of the group with the evident intention of ousting Sir Eustace from her side. Justin was quite used to seeing men fall over themselves to reach his rogue of a niece, and found the spectacle highly diverting. Glancing at Rogers, he saw that this amusement was far from being shared.

After a few moments Lady Marton said that they really must return to the carriage to see how poor George was faring, and her party moved away.

"Don't forget," murmured Sir Eustace in Anthea's ear, as they separated, "I shall be waiting here."

A demure smile, and she turned away to walk beside Louisa and their aunt, with Justin and Rogers bringing up the rear.

Two races had been run before Anthea's original impulse returned. Caught up in the excitement of seeing which horse would win as the animals thundered round the track, for a time she was sufficiently diverted.

During the interval before the third race, however, the urge returned, and she gained her aunt's permission for Louisa and herself to walk about a little. Justin and Rogers had already moved off to have a word with Harry, who had come to the Races with some friends of his own age. She saw them in the crowd as she and Louisa made their way along, but carefully avoided them.

Her only difficulty now, she thought urgently, was Louisa. She knew her cousin would never agree to accompany her to the fortune-teller's booth, but she could not possibly leave the girl on her own at a race meeting. To her delight, she suddenly espied Louisa's admirer Mr Giles Crispin strolling along with a lady whom she vaguely recognised from the wedding as his mother.

She drew Louisa's attention to the pair just as the gentleman had evidently seen them, for he started towards them with Mrs Crispin in tow.

"Louisa," she whispered, hurriedly, "pray don't make any remark if I leave you with these people after a few minutes. They will escort you back to Aunt Julia, I am sure."

"But — but where are you going?" Louisa asked, in agitated tones. "Pray, Anthea, don't get into a scrape, I implore you!"

There was no time for more, as the Crispins were face to face with them. Anthea was able to excuse herself from their company in a very short time, elatedly making her way to the fairground.

Sir Eustace was there, just as he had promised. For a moment, Anthea's maturer judgement questioned her impulsive actions; but she dismissed the intruding thought with a shrug, smiling provocatively at Knowle in a way which made him decide to follow up this happy meeting with others, more intimate.

They were admitted by an underling to the fortune-teller's presence in an aura of mystery. The interior was hung about with dark curtains, so that only the light from a shaded lantern cast a dim glow over a table in the centre. A large crystal ball, many faceted, had pride of place here. Over it brooded a veiled figure in dark, flowing robes and a head-dress in Eastern style. The figure gestured to them to be seated on two chairs at the opposite side of the table from herself. Anthea perched on the edge of hers, leaning forward curiously to study the crystal globe.

Petula, Queen of the Gipsies, began

to utter the usual small talk of fortune-tellers, in a deep, gutteral voice that might have been female or male. A journey, a dark stranger (Sir Eustace was fair to mid-brown) whom Anthea should not trust, a letter, a pleasant surprise, a happy marriage; everything a young lady might be supposed to desire. Anthea drank it all in, chuckling to herself, yet, in spite of this, trying to apply the prognostications to her own circumstances.

Sir Eustace openly laughed.

Petula turned a baleful eye upon him, leaning forward over the table in almost a threatening attitude.

"I see danger!" she hissed. "Dark danger, honourable gentleman, which will come upon you out of the past! Beware, beware, lest ye should not escape retribution!"

"What the devil — !"

Sir Eustace leapt to his feet. At that same moment, the dark curtain beside him was seared with flame. It quickly spread to the other hangings.

The Gipsy Queen jumped up and made good her escape through an unseen rear exit. At the same moment, Sir Eustace seized Anthea's hand and together they rushed for the entrance. Already the curtains concealing it were ablaze.

"Stand aside!" somebody from outside shouted.

Anthea recognised the combined voices of Justin and Rogers. She hastily obeyed.

A bucket of water cascaded over the curtain, followed by another, extinguishing the flames near the entrance sufficiently for the two to escape.

Anthea ran straight into the waiting arms of Rogers.

"Oh, my dear!" he exclaimed, looking anxiously into her upturned face. "Are you hurt?"

By then, a crowd had gathered from the neighbouring sideshows. Eager hands wielded buckets filled from a nearby horse trough, until all the flames were extinguished and the interior of the booth resembled a duck-pond.

Recollecting herself, Anthea withdrew from the shelter of Rogers's arms, blushing deeply.

"No, not the least little bit," she assured him, somewhat breathlessly.

Justin hailed Watts, who had that moment appeared on the scene. The Runner had been keeping general surveillance inside the enclosure, but hearing the commotion outside, he hastened there.

"What's happened, guv'nor?" he demanded.

"Damned if I know. Perhaps my niece can tell us. She crept off to visit this fortune-teller, and I got wind of it from her cousin, Miss Harvey, so came in pursuit accompanied by Mr Rogers here. Always in some devilish scrape or another — she's the most outrageous girl! Yes, and I'd like to know where that fellow Knowle comes into it, too," he added, with a dangerous glint in his eye.

Sir Eustace was standing beside Anthea and Rogers, looking very much at a loss; for the moment these two were taken up with each other.

As Justin and Watts approached the trio, they all made some effort to appear normal.

"I take it you're not injured, Anthea?" began Justin. "Or you, Knowle?"

Both disclaimed.

"Then mebbe ye'll tell us what

happened, sir?" Watts demanded of Knowle. "I'm a Bow Street Runner, understand."

"Damme if I know," replied Sir Eustace, with attempted nonchalance. "Saw Miss Rutherford about to enter the booth, so thought it best to escort her," The look that passed between him and Anthea was not lost on either Watts or Justin. "The fortune-teller's table and seats were surrounded by dark curtains, so couldn't see much. We both sat down, and this female started spoutin' some devilish fustian — you know the kind of thing! All at once, the hangings were on fire — God knows how — and the old witch vanished. I seized Miss Rutherford's hand and made a bolt for it. That's about all I can tell you."

Watts nodded. "Yes, thankee, sir." He turned to Justin. "I'll find this fortune-teller and then question some of the other show folk. Accident or arson, I wonder? Dare say ye'll want to know what I turn up, guv'nor?"

"Yes, indeed. I'm escorting Miss Rutherford to the grandstand, but I'll look out for you afterwards."

Taking the hint that his company was not wanted, Knowle parted from the others with a few words and a casual bow.

"That fellow seems on pretty easy terms with you after a very short acquaintance," Justin said to Anthea accusingly.

She tossed her head. "Oh, pooh, pray don't be so stuffy, dear Uncle! He's prodigiously amusing, which is more than may be said for some people!"

Rogers looked stung, but Justin laughed. "Ay, dare say he is — I'm sufficiently acquainted with men of his kidney to warn you to avoid them, my dear, but that I know it would only have the opposite effect," he replied, lightly. "Tell me, did it all happen as he said?"

"More or less," she said, in the same tone.

He looked at her sharply, guessing there had been some kind of assignation between Knowle and herself. No matter; he knew Anthea was quite able to make her admirers toe the line, flirt though she might.

He nodded. "You didn't see how the curtains caught fire?"

"No, we were concentrating on that crystal ball on the table, and listening to what the fortune-teller was saying! You know, Justin, of course it's all nonsense, but it's surprising how sometimes it seems to fit!"

He laughed again. "That's the art of it. Well, perhaps Watts will throw some light on the matter. Meantime, I recommend you should remain with the others."

She looked demure, and promised she would.

Watts had very little information to offer when he and Justin met later. He had found Petula; the Queen of the Gipsies turned out to be a dark visaged man of short stature.

"He was quaffin' ale with some of the other showmen, sir, swearing powerful, like, about the damage. Reckons it was done by a lad he gave a hiding to yesterday for snoopin' around his booth. No sign o' the lad now — well, wouldn't be. One odd thing, though."

He paused, frowning.

"What?" queried Justin, encouragingly.

"Mebbe it's of no account, guv'nor. But he let slip that someone had greased his fist to say certain things to the gennelman who was with Miss Rutherford — words of warning, or some such gammon. Seems by eye witness accounts that this Knowle gennelman was hangin' about near the booth for some time afore the lady turned up."

"Was he, now? Just as I suspected — it was an arrangement between them, the little vixen! Could the fortuneteller give a description of the person who bribed him, male or female?"

"Male, sir. But that's about all he could tell me," replied Watts, disgustedly. "Seems members o' the public never notice what other folk look like, unless they happen to be covered in scars or warts, or else they're cripples. Always the same — makes a Runner's life mortal hard, sir."

"True. Well, it may have no connection with the fire, as you say. In any case, this is scarcely a crime for a man of your standing, Joe — more for the parish constable. D'you happen to know what won the last race? I missed it, looking after my niece's concerns."

* * *

Knowle stifled a yawn as he bent over the billiard table to study the angle for his next shot. There were plenty of gaming houses in York, as he well knew, but a lamentable lack of funds prevented his patronising them at present. When he had been here a few days longer, it would be possible to touch his sister for some blunt; but best not to do it straight away, under his brother-in-law's hostile eye. In the meantime, it was either a game of billiards or bezique with that same prosy fellow, as an after dinner pastime.

Tomorrow, thank God, they would be dining out, by Mrs Cholmondley's invitation. He smiled as he thought of exchanging a dull, boring evening like this for the stimulation of a little light dalliance with that fascinating rogue, Anthea Rutherford, who would also be present. And, after all, tomorrow's visit to the Races might prove more profitable than today's, which had cleaned him out of what meagre funds he had possessed. He was nothing if not an optimist.

The evening dragged on, enlivened

only by the ritual tea drinking with his sister Mary just after ten o'clock. Conversation was of the day's winners and the prospects for tomorrow, until it switched to domestic matters. This brought on a severe attack of Eustace's yawns again.

"I declare you're monstrous tired!" said Mary, sympathetically. "It must be all the fresh air at the Races. I dare say you're not accustomed to being so much out of doors — you were never a keen sportsman."

"No," agreed her spouse cynically. "More of a club man, shall we say?"

"Say what you like," retorted Eustace, indifferently. "Think I'll take a stroll on the terrace before retiring. I'll say goodnight now."

Mary de Ryde rose to her feet to plant a sisterly kiss on his cheek. He suffered it, recognising the need to turn the old girl up sweet, as he put it mentally. Philip contented himself with a nod and an answering cool goodnight. The fellow could go to the devil for all he cared.

The small family drawing room was on the ground floor, with French windows leading on to the terrace. Eustace opened one and stepped outside, closing it after him.

He took a few turns about the terrace, trying to throw off his mood of boredom. The quiet domestic life was not for him, he thought, which was why he had never fallen into Parson's Mousetrap. Not that if an heiress had come in his way he would not have snapped her up quickly, be she never so plain. But hopeful mamas had a shrewd trick of smelling out a fortune-hunter, so he had never got past their guard. He had almost given up the chase in recent years, though there had been other females in plenty. He shrugged. Perhaps he might have the luck soon to come in the way of a rich widow who would yield to his charm. Women invariably did. Come to think of it, Harrogate or Cheltenham would be ideal places for such an encounter, could he but raise the wind for a visit. Spas invariably attracted widows.

The moon was up, and the garden presented a pleasing aspect even to one who was no lover of Nature. Now if only there had been some attractive female at his side — say Anthea Rutherford — he would have been tempted to wander along these moonlit walks. He ran lightly down the steps and turned along the path directly under the wall of the terrace. A large statue of some Roman warrior stood a short way along. He fancied he detected a movement behind it, and paused, his eyes focusing on the point. Seeing nothing more, he attributed the fancy to the effect of moonlight, and went on past the statue.

Suddenly a figure leapt out at him, and he knew no more.

7

"NASTY," said Runner Watts.

Dr Clent agreed, looking down dispassionately at the battered head of the corpse lying at his feet.

"Murder," he said, "and the weapon to hand."

He lifted a jagged lump of stone which had broken off the plinth of the statue at some time. Ominous dark stains covered its surface.

The body had been found early that morning by an under gardener, who had rushed quaking to his superior. This worthy had at once declared Sir Eustace Knowle 'a goner' before alerting the household. Philip de Ryde had summoned the doctor, who confirmed this diagnosis, adding that as it was undoubtedly murder, the body had best be left *in situ* until the authorities had taken a look. Soon the parish constable and Runner Watts were on the scene, joined by Justin Rutherford who had been asked by his brother-in-law to act as deputy for him in his role as magistrate.

Watts nodded. "Not premeditated, shouldn't opine," he offered, looking at Justin. "We're told he took a stroll outdoors on impulse about eleven o'clock. Who was to know he'd do that? Couldn't hardly lie in wait for him on the off-chance."

Justin frowned. "True. One wonders, though, about this Gipsy's warning you mentioned yesterday at the Races? A coincidence, most likely — did the fortune-teller give you the message verbatim?"

"No, guv'nor." Watts shook his head. "A warning, that's all he said. But them gentry are as full o' warnings as an egg is of meat — stock in trade, that is. Only thing caught my attention was that another party had put the gipsy up to it. You don't think, sir — ?"

"No knowing. I'll ask my niece if she can repeat the message. Meantime, perhaps we can authorise the relatives to remove the body for decent burial, pending the official inquest, of course."

Dr Clent parted from them to see what could be done to alleviate the grief of Mrs de Ryde, who sincerely mourned her scapegrace brother. Meanwhile Justin and Joe Watts sought out the lady's husband to ask him a few more questions.

They found him rather less than prostrated by grief, although he murmured that it was a shocking business.

"Most likely the poor fellow disturbed some intruder," he added.

"Ay, so it would appear, sir," agreed Watts. "Especially in view of these robberies that have been taking place hereabouts recently. Not that the murderer filched aught from the unfortunate gennelman — his watch, fob, seals and pocket book were all there, right and tight. But most like he scarpered quick when he saw his man was a goner."

Justin nodded. "All the same, Mr de Ryde, it is perhaps worth asking if your brother-in-law had any enemies?"

Philip de Ryde grimaced, and glanced at the Bow Street Runner as if reluctant to say too much in front of him.

"I knew little of his private life. He

rarely visited us, and then only for short periods — when his pockets were to let, I fear." He smiled deprecatingly. "One might say he was a rolling stone. He was mostly in London, but his infrequent letters to my wife seldom came from the same place."

"I see. Any close friends who might know more?"

The other shook his head. "It would surprise me to learn that he had any. His borrowing habits must have alienated all of 'em. He made mention of a group of gambling, carousing fellow-spirits whom he hobnobbed with from time to time, but no one name comes especially to mind. Used to patronise the gambling hells rather than White's or Brooks's — sure way to end at point non plus, as I don't need to tell you. Ah, well — *de mortuis*, I suppose."

Justin rose. "Thank you, sir," he said, with a short bow. "There seems small likelihood that the attack was a personal one, but it was worth considering."

It seemed to him that de Ryde looked thoughtful for a moment, but nothing was said as he accompanied them personally through the hall to the main entrance.

A maid, obviously one of the upper servants, was also passing through hurriedly, but she stopped stock still on seeing them. Her eyes widened in horror and she let out a low moan as she clung, half fainting, to the newel post at the foot of the stairway.

The three men halted, eyebrows raised in surprise. The butler, who hovered close behind his master as he was seeing the guests out, clicked his tongue impatiently and moved towards the woman.

"Now, now, Healey, what's all this?" he asked, reproachfully. "*You'd* best not be setting yourself up with hysterics! Pull yourself together, do, and get along to your mistress! She needs you."

"That — that man with the master," she whispered, in a tone that only just reached their listening ears. "Is he — is he — the Runner from Bow Street they've been talking of?"

The butler nodded. "Yes, but he needn't concern you, silly widgeon! Now get along, do, like I said."

"Oh, my Gawd!"

She let the exclamation slip involuntarily

before taking a deep breath, pulling herself upright, and scurrying out of the hall through a service door.

"I apologise for Healey, sir," said the butler, placatingly. The staff are all at sixes and sevens, I fear."

"Understandable," said de Ryde.

Once outside, Justin and Watts exchanged glances.

"Seems your phiz strikes terror into the most innocent heart," Justin remarked, grinning at his companion. "Mind, I don't blame the female — that proboscis of yours *is* a fearsome thing! All the same — natural shock arising from a murder on the premises, d'you think? Or was there some particular reason why she don't wish to see you?"

Watts grunted. "You will have your little jest, gov'nor! Wouldn't surprise me if she'd been up to something on her own account, not connected with the murder. Most folk who behave like that at sight o' me have got something to hide, though most times it's got no connection with my inquiry."

"Mm. Did you gain the impression, as I did, that our friend de Ryde was also keeping something back? Seemed to me that when I said we'd thought it worth checking the possibility of a personal attack on Knowle — "

"He looked no how for a moment — yes, I did, guv'nor. Wonder what there is behind that?"

Justin shrugged. "As you say, most people keep something back when confronted by officialdom, often for trivial reasons. We'll report to Sir George in due form and see what he has to say."

* * *

"Odd, that business of the warning," said Sir George, frowning. "You say that by Anthea's account, this gipsy uttered a warning about danger out of the past, and retribution? That's devilish strange, y'know, Justin, I must say."

"Any particular reason why you should say so, George?"

The two men were closeted together in the library, Watts having withdrawn for refreshment into the servants' hall. Justin had first spoken to his niece, who had given him an accurate report of the gipsy's words. She was naturally shocked at the news of Sir Eustace Knowle's murder; but as their acquaintance had been so recent, the effect was passing, and her curiosity quickly came to the fore. Somewhat to her chagrin, she had been barred from the interview with her Uncle George.

Sir George was silent for a moment, and Justin repeated the question. The other man eased his injured ankle into a more comfortable position on the footstool before replying, a slightly hangdog expression on his face.

"Fact is, I received a letter the other day with some similar damned tarradiddle! Anonymous, of course, and hadn't come through the post, though it was amongst the rest of my correspondence on the desk here." He waved a hand towards it. "I questioned the footman who'd picked up the post from the village receiving office, but it was plain he could tell me nothing. I meant to go down to the office to question the postmaster, Ned Appleton, but what with one thing and another — "

"Did you by any chance keep that letter, George?" asked Justin, sharply.

"Yes, for I meant to follow it up. If you open that left hand top drawer you should find it — I simply tossed it in."

Justin rose, crossed over to the desk and opened the drawer, removing the folded paper which rested inside. The superscription was to Sir George Marton, Firsdale Hall, written in capitals. He opened it out, reading carefully the message it contained.

"Hm!" he said, judicially, having mastered the contents. "The writer evidently finds you one of the poorest specimens of humanity, and intends to avenge himself upon you for an injury in the past. Any notion, old chap, what that injury might be?"

Sir George shrugged. "Devil a bit. Y'know how it is, though, Justin — in the execution of my duties as a magistrate I bring wrong-doers to justice. Any one of 'em might decide to avenge himself — who's to say?"

"Most serious offenders who appear before you would either be hanged — in which case they could scarcely seek vengeance! — or else transported. And this must have been a serious business, one feels, to come to murder. Murder of Knowle, though, not you." Justin broke off, frowning. "It would seem," he went on, slowly, "that vengeance is being sought for something in which both of you were involved at some time in the past. Can you cast your mind back to recall any such affairs?"

"I and *Knowle*? Good God, I scarce know the man — that's to say, *knew* of course. I saw him on occasion when he was staying at Denby House — as you know, de Ryde and I have been friends and neighbours for I don't know how long — but my acquaintance with his brother-in-law was of the sketchiest kind. Didn't like the man, to own truth! He never came to Denby House unless he was sponging on his sister, and de Ryde didn't like it above half. He'd have kicked him out, but for his wife's sake."

Justin nodded. "So I collected from what he said to me earlier. There's nothing, then, that could connect you and the murdered man as objects of some felon's vengeance? No case that came before you in which Knowle was involved?"

Sir George began to shake his head, then he stopped suddenly.

"Wait a moment, though! Yes, it's coming back to me, now! A devil of a time ago, it would be — something to do with a servant of Knowle's stealing a family heirloom from the de Rydes while he and his master were staying there! Can't recall the servant's name, but he was found guilty and transported for fourteen years. Yes, and he persisted in arguing in his defence that Knowle had put him up to it, but that didn't fadge, of course."

Justin's eyes glinted in the way they had when his interest was caught.

"Hah! Now that does sound as though it might have a connection! Fourteen years — that would take us back to 1802. It will be on record, of course, if we can discover the date of the trial and the man's name. Doubtless de Ryde can give us that information, though dare say he won't be best pleased to see me back again."

"I would go myself, old chap," said Sir

George, apologetically, "but this damned ankle makes any kind of transport uncomfortable, to say the least. Besides, although it's my job to inquire into any nefarious matters in the locality, murder is an affair for Bow Street, and we're fortunate enough to have a Runner at hand. Not to mention, of course — " he shot Justin a sly look — "your own considerable prowess in solving puzzles of the kind."

Justin grinned. "You are too good. But speaking of puzzles, when did you receive this warning letter — " he tapped the paper which he was still holding — "before or after your so-called accident?"

His brother-in-law let out a whistle, then nodded.

"Must admit, that thought had crossed my mind. Before — in fact, the previous day, day of the masquerade. Think it was deliberate do you?"

"Not much doubt of it. You wouldn't talk about it at the time — don't blame you for that, with Julia and the other females present — but suppose you go over the incident for me now, in as much detail as you can possibly recollect?"

Marton obliged, protesting as he did so that there was little to relate.

"You're sure there were no birds flying near?" insisted Justin.

"Not a single one, though the noise of the shot put up a few afterwards."

"Did you hear any movement in the wood before the shot? Or any other shots as you approached?"

"Can't say that I did. I wasn't paying any particular heed, mind, as my thoughts were on the business I had with Thwaite, my tenant."

"Who would have known you'd be riding that way?"

Sir George shrugged. "Thwaite, for one, as we had an appointment. Anyone in the household might have done. Look, Justin, what are you suggesting? That someone knew I'd be going that way, and lay in wait for me?"

"Something of the kind."

"But that's absurd! My own servants! Or Thwaite, who's been my tenant for I don't know how long!"

"I seem to recall," replied Justin, frowning in an effort of memory, "that

Sprog and I were about to set out for Sheriff Hutton at the same time as you went off to see your tenant farmer. We all met at the stables, and announced our plans in front of the grooms. And, yes! Didn't you remark that one of 'em was new, you'd not seen him before? Your head groom explained that he'd taken on a couple of new hands for the wedding, I believe."

"Damme if you're not right!" exclaimed Sir George. "There *was* a strange face, and Carr said there were two of 'em — gave me their names, but they just slip my memory at present. But that's all gammon, m'dear chap — must be! Carr wouldn't engage anyone without being very careful about references. Typical canny Yorkshireman, y'know."

"Mm," said Justin, unconvinced. "Well, references *can* be forged, though I'm not saying these were. I'll get Watts to look into it, also find out where those new stable-hands went that day. But the so-called accident begins to look a trifle smokey, don't you agree?"

"Well, yes, but there's one point you've overlooked. If the unknown marksman was out to kill me, why didn't he? Even supposing he missed first shot, there was ample opportunity when I came off Rowley."

"Yes, I had thought of that, as a matter of fact, and I don't know the answer," admitted Justin. "Mayhap he was only out to scare you, possibly he was interrupted in some way — we can't know without more evidence. Nevertheless, I think you should take care for the future, until we discover Knowle's murderer — if we do. Meanwhile, I'll see what further light de Ryde may be able to throw on the matter."

* * *

As Justin had anticipated, Philip de Ryde gave him a cool reception, stating at once that he could add nothing to what had already been said, and therefore could see little point in going over it all again.

"Quite so, sir," Justin agreed, "but this is about another matter altogether, though not, we think, unconnected with your brother-in-law's murder."

He began to explain. When he made

mention of the threatening letter that Sir George Marton had received prior to his accident, Philip de Ryde gave a convulsive start.

"Good God! D'you say so? Eustace threatened by a gipsy — Marton also threatened! I must tell you, Rutherford, that I, too, received a note couched in such terms — it was delivered to me the morning after the Lord Mayor's masquerade ball! I'd no intention of saying anything about it to anyone, but this alters matters."

"Now that is most interesting, and bears out a theory which I have about this unsavoury business. Tell me, has any attempt been made upon your life since then?"

"Attempt upon — " de Ryde broke off in dismay.

After a pause he spoke again, more calmly.

"So you believe that whoever killed Eustace has designs not only upon Marton's life, but upon mine? But it don't make sense — why?"

"It could do if you consider who might bear a strong grudge against all three of you," replied Justin. "I put the question to George, and he recalled an incident many years ago which involved the theft of a valuable necklace belonging to Mrs de Ryde. The thief was a servant of your late brother-in-law, who was staying with you at the time. The man was charged, found guilty, and transported. Do you recall this?"

"Good God! Of course I do! I could scarce forget a furore of that kind! The most damnable thing!"

"Quite so. Perhaps you'd be good enough to give me some detailed information, sir? This man, for instance — was he an old servant of Sir Eustace's?"

Philip de Ryde snorted. "He didn't possess any old retainers, for the simple reason that he never paid their wages. As I remember, he told us that this fellow was an out-of-luck minor actor who'd been glad to take service with him as a valet and general factotum. He brought the man from London with him on that particular occasion — the usual repairing lease, I fear."

Justin nodded. "Can you perhaps recall

the man's name, and the actual date of the theft?"

Philip de Ryde frowned in an effort of concentration.

"It occurred in the spring of — let me see — 1803? No, 1802, I believe, for my daughter Anne had but just celebrated her second birthday, and she's sixteen now. As for the man's name — no, I couldn't hazard a guess. Y'know how it is with other people's servants, especially of a temporary kind. Tell you what, though, Rutherford, some of my own domestic staff may remember. After all, most of 'em have been with me ever since my marriage — butler, cook, housekeeper, my wife's personal maid, several of the outdoor staff. Have a word with Kirby, my butler — I'll send for him."

"Thank you. And I wonder if you'd mind my seeing him on his own? The man may be reluctant to answer questions freely in your presence."

"Not at all," agreed de Ryde.

"Perhaps you could prepare him a little for the substance of the interview? It might be preferable to springing the matter on him suddenly."

Philip de Ryde also thought this a good notion; so he went in search of Kirby, the butler, in person, rather than summoning him to the room.

Kirby was a comfortably portly man, with an almost totally bald head and shrewd eyes which missed nothing. The younger among the footmen serving under him knew better than to play off any tricks in front of their superior, although he was never unduly harsh with them.

Justin liked the look of the man, and judged he would be a useful informant.

"Mr de Ryde will have told you what this is about, Kirby," he began, "so I'll waste no more of your time in leading up to it. I'm anxious to learn all I can about this valet who stole the necklace, and the exact circumstances of the theft. Perhaps it would be best if you told the story in your own way, and I'll put questions to you when necessary."

"Very good, sir." Kirby gave a short bow. "The master was unable to recall the man's name, but I can, perfectly. It was Pringle. He was in his early twenties, quite a well-favoured fellow — or so the females seemed to think," he added, dryly. "In fact, he could twist them around his finger, and that was part of the trouble. Healey, the mistress' maid, was particularly taken with him."

Justin nodded, encouraging him to continue.

"They got very thick together, those two. He was a Londoner, of course. Very good sort of folk, I dare say — " a note of scepticism crept in here — "but smoother in manner than our local lads and lasses. Or perhaps it was because he'd been an actor. Not much of one, by what I could make out, at least as far as getting jobs was concerned, but able to tell the tale, all right and tight. Healey, poor wench, was fair dazzled by him, for all she's almost ten years older and might have been supposed to have more sense. But there, what female ever does where a personable man's in question?"

Justin grinned in acknowledgement of this.

"She often allowed him to go into madam's dressing room, so naturally he knew where all the valuables were kept, and also the key to them. It came out in evidence later that he was used to frequenting shady pawnbrokers in London's more dubious quarters, though no felony had ever been brought home to him before. No doubt he meant to make off with the necklace back to London, where he'd know how best to dispose of it. But he caught cold at that, for madam suddenly decided to wear it at a ball on the very day that it was purloined, before he had a chance to escape. There was all Bedlam let loose when Healey reported it was missing, as you may suppose, Mr Rutherford."

"What occurred then?" asked Justin. "Did they send for the constable?"

"Yes, sir, and for the magistrate, Sir George Marton, as well. All the servants' rooms were searched, and it was discovered in Pringle's. He'd made small push to hide it, for it was lying quite openly in the top drawer of his dressing chest. Doubtless he hadn't had time to find a safer place of concealment."

"It isn't known precisely when it was taken?"

"No, sir, for madam and Healey, the maid, had been in York for the most of the day at madam's modiste. Pringle might easily have had access to the dressing room at any time during their absence. Sir Eustace was a very easy master — between his rising at about eleven o'clock and retiring, often in the small hours, Pringle was free to come and go as he chose."

"I collect that Mrs de Ryde wasn't in the habit of wearing that particular piece of jewellery frequently? Otherwise surely this fellow Pringle would have known that it wasn't safe to purloin it on a day when there was to be a ball? One supposes that he would have heard about the ball. No doubt Sir Eustace would have been attending it, too, as a guest in the house."

Kirby nodded. "You are in the right of it on both counts, sir," he acknowledged. "He certainly knew about the ball, but Healey herself didn't know that madam was to wear the necklace, as she never did so unless pressed by the master. It is a family heirloom, heavy and old fashioned, and the mistress makes no secret of the fact that she detests it, and thinks it unbecoming. All this

Pringle would have learnt from Healey, so he must have felt himself quite safe in choosing that particular piece. Its loss wouldn't have been discovered for months — perhaps years — if madam hadn't suddenly taken a notion to wear it. And as Sir Eustace was leaving for London on the following day, taking Pringle with him, the villain would have come off safely enough. Likely he'd have disappeared once back in London."

Justin knitted his brows thoughtfully.

"And Healey presumably was not guilty of complicity in the theft?" he asked. "Sir George Marton must have been satisfied of that when he undertook the preliminary investigation, otherwise she, too, would have been charged."

Kirby smiled wryly. "Sir George opined that she was a foolish widgeon who'd doted on the man, and let him use her, so he didn't bring her to justice."

"I see. Sir George mentioned to me that in his defence Pringle stated that his master had initiated the scheme for stealing the necklace. Do you recall anything about that?"

Kirby shifted uncomfortably. "Well, he

would, sir, wouldn't he? There wasn't much else he could find to say."

"It *is* a fairly obvious gambit," agreed Justin.

He paused for a moment, then asked delicately, "Do you consider it could be, let us say, within the bounds of possibility?"

Kirby's discomfort deepened.

"Well, sir, there's no denying Sir Eustace — speak no ill of the dead — was a bright spark, and always in Dun territory. He might — mind I don't say he did, Mr Rutherford — but he *might* have thought, him being short of blunt and madam always ready to loose her purse strings for him, that he'd borrow the necklace, so to speak, pop it, and then recover it when he was in funds again. He knew she hated it and rarely wore it, so she wouldn't be likely to miss it before he could get it back. And this valet of his being in the know with shady pawnbrokers — well, sir, it's just what *might* have happened. No saying it did," he added, quickly.

"Mm." Justin pondered for several minutes, while the butler stood deferentially by, waiting for dismissal. At last, his glance came back into focus again.

"Thank you, Kirby, I'm much obliged to you for your help. Would you be good enough to send Healey to me? I believe a word with her might be useful."

But this part of the investigation had to be postponed. Kirby returned to report that Healey could not be spared at present from attendance on her mistress, who had taken her brother's death hard and required the ministrations of both her medical man and the maid.

"When do you think I can have a word with your wife's maid?" asked Justin, as Philip de Ryde escorted him to the door. "She may have valuable information to add to what Kirby has already supplied. It seems she was much involved with this fellow Pringle."

"So she was, but it's a long time since, and I expect she'll have put the whole wretched business behind her now. Still, if you think she can assist you in discovering this villain — always supposing your theory is correct, though I must say, my dear Rutherford, it does sound highly improbable. I trust you take no offence," he added, in a conciliatory tone.

"Not the least in the world," Justin assured him, cheerfully. "There is one other possible explanation, and that is the existence of some kind of local vendetta which involves others of your neighbours. There's to be a dinner party this evening at the house of your neighbour Cholmondley, I believe — that is, unless it's cancelled because of the murder. Naturally you won't be there, in any event, but my relatives have already accepted, and I shall prime George to ask the men if they've received any threatening letters. It can probably be done quietly, perhaps after the ladies leave us to our wine. In the meantime, Mr de Ryde, I'd recommend you to have a care. And perhaps you'll be good enough to let me know of the first opportunity for questioning your wife's maid, Healey."

8

"REVENGE!" exclaimed Anthea, with a shudder. "How prodigiously Gothic! Do you truly think so, Justin?"

She had been listening spellbound, together with Rogers, to Justin's account of the interviews at Denby House.

"It certainly seems a strong possibility," said Rogers, "if there's anything in the butler's speculation about the late baronet's part in the theft. Lud, I can just imagine that valet of his nursing revenge for all those horrendous years in a convict settlement in Australia — don't bear thinking of! Except I collect he was no innocent, but a pretty hardened malefactor who'd been lucky enough not to get caught before. All the same, not a pin to choose between master and man, if the accounts are accurate."

Justin nodded. "George is confident from the evidence that came out at the trial that Pringle was undoubtedly a wrong 'un. But *if* Knowle instigated the crime and stood to gain most from it, then the valet would certainly have cause to feel aggrieved that he should shoulder all the blame. As you say, Sprog, the rancour would grow with the years of misery. I don't doubt, myself, that the butler's taken Knowle's measure correctly. An upper servant is a pretty reliable judge of character when it comes to his own household."

"Oh, one wouldn't have trusted him," agreed Anthea. "He was too plausible by half."

"Yet you seemed very well pleased with him," said Rogers, somewhat stiffly.

"I, too, have moments of dissimulation," she replied, with a saucy twinkle. "But Justin — " turning to him — "I don't quite see why Uncle George and Mr de Ryde should have been threatened as well? Oh, I suppose Uncle George because he was the magistrate who brought Pringle to trial — but why Mr de Ryde?"

"To hazard a guess, if Kirby suspected Knowle's part in the theft, so would de Ryde. He'd obviously got no illusions about his brother-in-law. Naturally he kept quiet at the time about any suspicions he had, and I surmise that the valet would harbour a grudge against him on that account." He frowned. "It's a pity that I couldn't see the maid Healey this morning. I feel she may have more light to shed on the business."

"That reminds me," said Anthea, suddenly. "When I was walking with Fanny to Denby House on Sunday afternoon, she told me some rigmarole about Anne de Ryde having surprised Healey going through her mother's bureau. I don't suppose there could be any connection — "

"Mm," said Justin, thoughtfully. "When Watts and I went over to Denby House earlier, this woman Healey passed by us in the hall, and seemed ready to swoon when she realised Watts was from Bow Street. The butler excused her on the grounds of the murder, but Watts and I did wonder if there might be anything else. It begins to be urgent that I should see her, I think."

"Oh, do let me accompany you!" begged Anthea, eagerly. "After all, this needs a woman's touch!"

"No fear!" replied Justin, laughing. "In my view, this is more a matter for Watts. He's a deal of expertise in questioning servants. Never mind — " as her face fell — "I don't doubt I shall need to call on your invaluable services at some time or other."

"I beg you won't!" almost snapped Rogers. "It's highly unsuitable, not to say dangerous, for Miss Anthea to embroil herself in this business!"

Justin gazed at him in mild surprise, but Anthea positively glared.

"And pray who gave you the right to interfere in *my* concerns?" she demanded.

He looked steadily at her before replying.

"I beg your pardon," he said at last, stiffly.

Shortly afterwards, with a brief excuse, he rose and quitted the room. Justin gave Anthea a comically reproachful look.

"There, you see you've quite overset Sprog! You do dole out Turkish treatment to the poor fellow!"

"It serves him right," retorted Anthea, "for presuming to dictate to me on matters of conduct! I will *not* allow even you — "

Justin wagged an admonitory finger at her, interrupting.

"Stuff, m'dear. I've often enough spiked your guns, and I'm still here to tell the tale. But Sprog will doubtless recover."

Anthea elevated her chin. "It is a matter of supreme indifference to me what he does," she declared.

Justin grinned. "Oh, yes, very true. Now, don't fly up into the boughs," he went on, hastily, "but do listen to my alternative theory about the murder. There's just a possibility — " as he saw that he had her attention — "of an outbreak of anonymous threatening letters in the neighbourhood written by some bedlamite who doesn't stop at threats. George's accident would fit as well into that theory as into the revenge motive. We mean to sound out the guests this evening at the Cholmondleys' party, and if you should chance to hear any gossip to the purpose — mind, though," he added, quickly, seeing her eyes light up — "*no* direct questions, is that understood? It might queer the whole pitch."

She nodded, docilely for Anthea.

* * *

The Chomondleys lived at Warton Manor, less than half a mile distant from Firsdale Hall and Denby House. They had been settled in the neighbourhood for ten or eleven years, having inherited the property from an aged relative who had never had much intercourse with his neighbours. Mr James Cholmondley at once set about rectifying this situation. Both he and his wife were easy going, uncritical people who liked company and possessed few relatives. Invitations went out to the whole neighbourhood at frequent intervals, and as it was impossible for people to find excuses all the time, their social occasions, though privately stigmatised as insipid, were reasonably well attended. In Races week especially, James Cholmondley would have a house full of long staying guests, as well as inviting his neighbours in to meet them. This year there were only half a dozen house guests, rather a poor showing, as Sir George remarked *sotto voce* to his wife. Three of these had been introduced to the Firsdale Hall party at the masquerade; of the others, a Mr and Mrs Thrixen from Helmsley were frequent visitors. The third was a stranger from the Midlands, a sporting gentleman named Reade who had failed to secure accommodation in York through a lack of foresight in booking, and been rescued by Cholmondley just when being turned away from one of the hotels.

"Couldn't possibly let him miss Races week, now could I?" said their host, as he introduced Mr Reade. "Plenty of room here — m' wife and I enjoy nothing better than entertaining."

Mr Reade, an agile looking man in his late thirties with the tanned countenance and sun bleached brown hair of one who spends most of his time out of doors, smiled and bowed to the newcomers.

"Deuced good of Cholmondley, though, what? Not many people as hospitable, don't y'know. I collect you're a sportsman yourself, sir — " to Sir George, nodding at the stick with which he was contriving to move around among the company — "and have, as I hear, taken a tumble recently. Deuced bad luck — I commiserate."

Sir George nodded in acknowledgment, but said nothing.

"I believe, though," put in Mr Barnet, in his rather flat tones, "that this wasn't an ordinary sporting accident, but something of a more sinister nature?"

"Sinister?" echoed Sir George sharply. "Pooh! Fustian, sir! I beg you won't discuss so trivial a matter!"

Barnet bowed, a cynical look in his eyes. Sir John Fulford exchanged a surreptitious wink with him. Evidently these two, at any rate, were better informed even than their host.

Meanwhile, Mrs Cholmondley was explaining to Julia Marton why she had not cancelled her evening party on hearing of the murder of Sir Eustace Knowle that morning.

"I trust you don't consider it too shocking of us, Lady Marton, but indeed we scarce knew the unfortunate gentleman — I suppose we may have met him once several years since at the de Rydes, but even for that I can't vouch, I assure you! And put-offs are so difficult at the last minute, and we only heard towards luncheon, then we thought it might be only a stupid rumour, until Sir John Fellowes came in from the village and told us that he'd heard there it was true, that the Bow Street Runner had been to Denby House with your brother, Mr Rutherford, to inquire into the shocking, foul deed! And I'm sure the half of our neighbours don't yet know about it, but Sir George asked my husband particularly not to talk of it here, nor to encourage others to gossip, which advice we have tried to follow."

"But murder will out," whispered Anthea to Louisa, unable to repress her all too ready sense of humour.

Julia Marton made a suitable reply to her voluble hostess and hastened to move on to other ladies in the room.

It was true that few of the people there had yet heard of the murder; but in spite of Sir George's attempts at discouragement, those in the know could not resist passing the information on to others. It was generally agreed, however, that it would be foolish to alarm the ladies at a social occasion, so the news was circulated quietly among the menfolk.

Justin found himself sought out as word went round that he had been with the Runner that morning to view the scene of the crime.

"Would you say, Mr Rutherford, that there's any fear we may have a homicidal maniac loose in the neighbourhood?" asked one of the guests, nervously. "Did the Bow Street man incline to that opinion?"

"Good God, no, Browne!" expostulated another. "Sounds to me more like a marauder waiting his chance to break into the house, and he lashed out when Sir Eustace Knowle surprised him. Don't forget, there've been a deal of burglaries around York of late. Good thing we've got a Runner handy, without the delay of sending to London for somebody."

"Rumour has it," put in Fulford, who had come up with Barnet and Reade to join Justin's group, "that you yourself, Rutherford, have something of a flair for solving mysteries. I was up in

London recently and heard your name in connection with the Jermyn affair."

"And pray what was that?" asked the man called Browne.

"Gentlemen, I beg you'll change the subject," warned Justin, hurriedly. "Here come some of the ladies, and this topic is hardly suitable for a social evening."

Fulford's eyes gleamed as he saw Anthea among the group approaching, and he promptly lost interest in the foregoing conversation, making his way to her side and doing his utmost to ingratiate himself with her.

She had little use for him, and would have turned him a cold shoulder; but she chanced to catch Rogers looking her way, so at once changed her mind. Her lively, flirtatious greeting quite surprised the gentleman, and earned her a contemptuous glance from the real object of her play. Justin caught her eye for a moment, and gave the slightest shake of his head. In answer, she tilted her chin and laughed even more often.

As previously agreed between Sir George and Justin, the matter of anonymous letters was broached in the interval after dinner when the men were sitting over their wine. An easy, relaxed time; and it was very much in that manner that Sir George began.

"Tiresome thing," he said, as he filled his glass and passed the decanter round, "but one of our neighbours has complained to me that he recently received an anonymous letter. Full of nonsense, of course, as such things usually are, but, as I say, tiresome. He asked me to look into it, see if anyone else had been troubled in the same way, with a view to laying hands on the culprit. So — if any of you *did* get such a letter recently, perhaps you'd be good enough to let me know? Better still, if you've kept it, I'd like to take a look."

He glanced round the table, apparently still relaxed, but in fact watching their faces keenly, as were also Justin and Rogers. Most shook their heads at once; some looked thoughtfully at Sir George, as though sensing something more than appeared on the surface. Cholmondley burst into excited speech, gabbling away as was his wont.

"Anonymous letters? Dear me, whatever next? As though a murder in the neighbourhood were not enough! But who was it who received this letter, Marton? Not anyone present, I collect, or you would have said so — but then, almost everyone who signifies *is* present, so who can it be?" He looked around him for some sign from one of the others, but seeing nothing, shrugged helplessly. "Well, *I* haven't had any such letters. Have any of the rest of you?"

He looked round the table again, and this time the head shaking was general.

"Capital!" he exclaimed, satisfied. "Y'see, Marton, it's simply one isolated incident, probably some servant who's been turned off and done it for spite. Yes, I should think that's most likely, wouldn't you? And no doubt you'll easily track the wretch down, and put a stop to the business. I don't know what this neighbourhood's coming to — burglaries, anonymous letters — though only the one, of course — and even murder! Yes, and a pickpocket at the Lord Mayor's masquerade in York, I'd forgotten that — though that's not *precisely* this neighbourhood, of course, not our *local* area. I wonder, my dear fellow — " turning to Barnet — "if that felon should have been the same one whom you were so clever as to prevent from robbing me? But I couldn't recall his face, could you? It was all too quick."

Barnet shook his head. "Plenty of them about."

The conversation was allowed to drift into more usual channels.

It was later, when Sir George had retired to the room set aside for gentlemen's cloaks, that he put his hand into his pocket and found a piece of paper.

Puzzled, he pulled it out and unfolded it. It contained a short message of only six words.

YOU ARE GUILTY AND SHALL DIE!

* * *

On the following morning Justin and Watts met in the grounds of the Hall before the family was astir, in order to compare notes, as they had previously arranged.

Watts began. "Those two grooms, guv'nor, Leckby and Ross. Their references are satisfactory on the face of it. Leckby from the Black Swan in Coney Street — easily checked, though I haven't had time yet — t'other man Ross worked at a gennelman's stable in Bradford, since sold up, which was why he left. Leckby was under Carr's eye all that day when Sir George was shot at, but Ross was sent out soon after Sir George rode off for the farm. His errand was to get a horse shoed at the blacksmith's. Took an unconscionable time about it, according to Carr, so I had a word myself with the smith. He says Ross left the nag there promptly, then went off, returning much later, but the smith can't say exactly how long. I asked round the village, but no one seems to have seen him about. After some wench, was the smith's guess, and I didn't disagree, though no one can suggest a likely moll. Well, could he have ridden off after Sir George to take a pot shot at him? Sir George had at least twenty minutes start according to Carr's timing.

If Ross knew of a short cut, mayhap — but he's supposed to be a stranger hereabouts. And he could hardly ride hell for leather after Sir George without attracting the gennelman's notice. Don't seem to me feasible, what d'ye reckon, guv'nor? Though as to what the man *was* about, well, I'll go on pursuing my inquiries, unless ye've anything more urgent for me. The long and the short of it is motive, though. Why should he want to harm Sir George?"

"As to that, there's motive enough," replied Justin, having listened without interruption. "I've a deal to tell, Joe."

He proceeded to relate everything he had learnt since parting from Watts on the previous day. At the conclusion, the Runner emitted a long, low whistle.

"It seems tolerably certain that we can dispense with the theory of a general outbreak of threatening anonymous letters," concluded Justin. "No reaction was registered to that suggestion yesterday evening, and three of us were keeping a close watch. Besides, I think most of those present would have wanted to assist Sir George in such a matter — no reason why not. So we're left with the alternative — a felon returned to England from transportation, determined to avenge himself on those he considers responsible for his conviction. One of these people is already dead, and our task is to make sure that he doesn't wreak his vengeance on the other two, Sir George and Philip de Ryde. Both have received threatening letters, and there's no doubt that the recent mishap to Sir George was either an abortive attempt at murder, or intended as a warning that the villain meant business. There's more yet, as far as Sir George is concerned. Last night, just before he left the party at Cholmondley's place, Warton Manor, he found another threatening letter in the pocket of his evening cloak. Here it is."

Watts scrutinised the paper, then whistled.

"Don't waste words, does he? But that does give us a lead, sir, wouldn't ye say? We know our man's in the neighbourhood somewhere, but if he's got into a room at Warton Manor, surely we can start by looking there? He'll be a newcomer, o' course."

"Yes to that, but we can't take too much for granted about your other notion. To begin with, the note may have been placed in the pocket of the cloak before Sir George left home. Again, with all the fuss of a social gathering and the servants fully occupied, any outsider could easily enter the premises unnoticed. So the field is wider than might appear. I think we must consider first what manner of man we're looking for. All we know is that he was in his early twenties at the time of the robbery, was personable, and had been an actor — also, of course, a valet of sorts. Devil take it, Joe, he might be able to pass himself off as either a servant or a gentleman, choose how!"

"He'll have had a rough time in Australia, though, sir, and he'll have the marks o' that about him. Not easy to pass for gentry, I'd say."

"He may have been one of the more fortunate who are issued after a certain time, with what is known as a ticket of leave for good conduct. I was told about this by an officer on furlough over here last year, a man on the staff of Colonel Macquarie, Governor of

New South Wales. It appears that such convicts are excused from working for the government or the settlers to whom they've been assigned, and are allowed to set up in business for themselves, if they possess a trade, or else to earn their living as free employees. It seems many of them eventually do very well for themselves. If our man passed several years of his transportation sentence in these easier circumstances, all traces of rigorous toil will have been obliterated, and he'll appear much as any normal Englishman. No, I fear we can't hope for any simple, rule-of-thumb guide to his identity. All we can be sure of is his age, and the fact that he'll be a newcomer to the district."

Joe Watts grunted. "Seems to me, guv'nor, we've got our work cut out. Either of those grooms, though, would fit the bill by that reckoning."

"I agree. I think Mrs de Ryde's maid may perhaps be able to offer us further assistance. She'll surely recall more about this fellow's appearance and any little personal quirks than a mere male such as Kirby, the butler. After all, they said she used to be sweet on the fellow. I'd like you to interview her, Joe — you've a winning way with females."

Watts grinned. "Mayhap with some, sir, but younger wenches than this Healey. Besides, she fair took fright at me yesterday. That don't promise well for getting aught out o' her, now, does it?"

"You'll contrive, I'll wager. In any event, she'll be much more reticent with me, as a member of the Quality. Off you go, then, and don't let de Ryde refuse you access to her. There's all the authority of Bow Street behind you. And I think perhaps it may be as well to find you a room in the village inn for emergencies, as well as your official booking at the Olde Starre in York. There's no saying where you'll be most wanted."

9

HEALEY tiptoed from her mistress's bedroom, closing the door softly behind her, and made her way to the servants' staircase. She had started on her descent when one of the housemaids came running upstairs, meeting her halfway.

"Mr Kirby's looking for you, Mrs Healey," said the girl, evidently enjoying some secret source of pleasure, judging by the expression on her face. "He wants to see you in the Hall as soon as maybe, so he says."

Healey surveyed her coldly. "Indeed! And what would he be wanting, or didn't he tell the likes of you?"

"I couldn't say, I'm sure," replied the other, smugly. "All I know is, he's got some kind of visitor with him. But best not keep him waiting, sithee."

Healey swept past her with a contemptuous look, and continued down several flights until she reached the servants' hall.

She entered, then stood still, staring. Kirby was sitting at the table with another man, but he turned and rose as she slowly approached.

"Ah, Healey," he said, quietly. "Mistress asleep, is she?"

She nodded mutely, her eyes fixed upon the other man. Now she recognised him as the Bow Street Runner she had seen yesterday. Panic surged up in her.

"Mr Watts here would like a few words with you, Healey," explained the butler, still gently, for he saw that she had turned pale. "He's an officer from Bow Street looking into the villainous business of Sir Eustace Knowle's murder, as I think you already know. Now, no need to get yourself into a state about it, but just answer his questions sensibly, there's a good wench."

"I don't know nothing — anything — about it!" she gasped, clenching her hands together.

"No, course not," replied Watts, soothingly, rising to set a chair for her a little distance from the table and facing the window. "Pray sit down, ma'am, and be at ease. I don't bite, y'know."

She paused for a moment, then seated herself. Watts turned his chair towards her and also sat down, signalling with a nod of the head to Kirby to make himself scarce.

"I'm hoping ye'll be able to help me, Mrs Healey — it is Mrs, I take it?"

"It's — it's a what d'you call it — courtesy title — the lower servants use," she answered, hesitantly at first, but gaining fluency as she continued. "I'm a spinster, truth to tell, so's Cook, but she's always called *Mrs* Sallis. It don't do for the lower orders to get above themselves."

"Quite right and proper," he murmured, approvingly, "so I'll call ye Mrs, too, then happen I'll mind to keep *my* place."

He grinned engagingly at her, and she relaxed a little, even producing a somewhat coy look.

"That's better," he went on, "now we begin to understand each other. What I want from you, m'dear, is for you to cast your mind back a few years — a good few years — and tell me what ye can recall about a certain incident and the persons concerned in that incident."

The frightened expression returned to her eyes.

"A — an — incident — from years back?" she echoed, in a whisper.

"No need to be alarmed, Mrs Healey. The incident I refer to was the theft of Mrs de Ryde's necklace in 1802, fourteen years since. I would like you to tell me all you remember about that and the thief — a valet called Pringle. I've had an account from Kirby, and he gave me to understand that you were on friendly terms with this Pringle — perhaps I could say, *very* friendly terms?"

She lost colour again, putting her hands up to her mouth in a distracted gesture. She made some attempt to speak, but no words came.

He studied her for a moment in silence, then rose to cross over to a wall cupboard, producing from it a couple of glasses and a bottle. Kirby had offered him hospitality earlier from the same source.

He poured a measure of the liquid into each glass, pressing one of them firmly into Healey's grasp and raising the other to his own lips.

"Drink that up," he commanded.

She obeyed, but her hand trembled so that a few drops trickled down her chin. He gestured that she should empty the glass completely, then removed it from her, turning his back while she mopped at the spilt liquid.

When he turned round again, she seemed to have recovered some of her poise. Evidently the brandy was going to work; he decided to press home his advantage.

"Now," he said. "Easy does it. No harm in a pretty young wench strikin' up a friendship with a personable young feller, that I can see — only natural. Tell me about it."

She stared back at him defiantly, but the fear had left her eyes.

"As you say, there was no harm. Mind, it's a long time since, and I can't say as I rightly recall much about it."

"Just tell me the little ye do recall," he said, persuasively.

"Well, Sir Eustace came here on what the gentlemen call a repairing lease — pockets always to let, that one," she put in, disparagingly. "And Madam as soft as butter with him, always giving him money, which made the Master as mad as fire — many's the quarrel I've overheard when I've been in the dressing room! Not that I ever listen at doors, mind you — I wouldn't have you think that!"

"Such a notion would never enter my head, I assure ye, Mrs Healey."

She cast him a suspicious glance which he returned with a mild expression. Soothed by the brandy, she was reassured, and continued.

"He'd been several times before, but never brought his own valet, relying on sharing the services of Mr Goddard with the master. He — Pringle — " she hesitated over the name — "hadn't been long with Sir Eustace. He wasn't a valet by rights, but an actor who'd been out of work so long, he was glad to turn his hand to anything genteel. Not that he got paid, except by fits and starts, but there was a roof over his head and victuals, so he didn't find it too bad a bargain."

"How long did Sir Eustace stay that time?"

She considered for a moment. "About six weeks, I reckon. He only ever stayed until his pockets were filled again."

"So both of you being young, and in the same line of service — your work and his would keep you both on the floor of the family bedrooms mostly — you became friendly?"

She nodded.

"And I dare say, being friendly, he'd now and then pop his head round the door when you were clearing away your mistress' jewellery and such like in her bedroom?"

He put the question as casually as he was able; but even so she stiffened.

"That's what the magistrate, Sir George Marton, tried to make me say!" she exclaimed, going red in the face. "And it was no such thing! If Pringle did poke around in there, and he must have done, to lift that necklace, it was none o' my doing! I'm as innocent as the day I was born, and that's Gawd's truth! And so I told him!"

All at once, her defiance crumpled, and she began to snivel.

"It's a lonely life, bein' lady's maid," she whimpered. "Only the butler and the housekeeper on my level, and them married, and Mr Goddard, of course, but he was older than me, and a starched up, frowsty thing, to boot. And when a young feller comes along, ready to have a bit of a laugh with a body — "

She broke off, sobbing.

"There, there," said Watts, soothingly. "I understand very well, m'dear, and I'm not accusing ye of aught. But tell me, what was this young chap like in looks? Handsome? Tall or short? What colouring?"

She dried her tears, and was silent for a moment. Then she darted a quick, frightened look at him.

"Why? Why d'ye want to know?" she gasped.

"Never mind that, but try to answer the question," replied Watts, more firmly.

"There's something ye're not tellin' me!" she accused him.

"And there's something ye're not telling *me*," he retorted. "I want a description of this man Pringle, if ye please, ma'am."

"I can't say — it was too long ago — all I know was he seemed a personable man — all the female staff thought so — "

"But ye surely must remember if he was tall or short, dark or fair," he persisted. "Come, now."

"As far as I recollect, he'd be a bit shorter than you, and his hair was middling brown."

"And his eyes? Don't tell me ye didn't notice the colour of his eyes?" His tone was insinuating.

She flushed. "They were a kind of blue grey," she said, grudgingly. "But Kirby could tell you all this, as well as me."

"Mebbe, but it's you I'm asking. Was there anything else ye noticed about him — any distinguishing marks, like a wart, or some such? Perhaps not on his face or hands, but elsewhere, for instance?"

"What are ye suggesting?" she shouted. "D'ye have the impudence to accuse me of — of — behavin' like a trollop? Get out o' here! I'll not put up with another minute o' this! Get out!"

She had risen to her feet, pushed away the chair and was rushing for the door when he started after her, grabbing her wrist.

"A moment," he said, grimly. "Have ye seen this man since his transportation — have ye seen him lately?"

It was a bow at a venture, but the arrow went home.

She gave a loud gasp, turned deathly pale, and collapsed in a heap at his feet.

"And there was no more to be got out of her at that time," reported Watts to Justin, less than an hour later. "What with the cook and a gaggle o' housemaids with sal volatile and burnt feathers, you never knew such a commotion goin' on, guv'nor, not since we was in the Peninsula with Old Hookey — beggin' his pardon, the Duke o' Wellington — an' Boney's lot were pepperin' us! I scarpered double quick, and so did the butler. But I'll have another touch at her, never fear. I reckon she knows something."

* * *

Anne de Ryde had been paying small attention to the Elegant Extracts which her governess Miss Fawcett had set her to copy. She kept biting the end of her pen and staring into space, from time to time, fetching heartfelt sighs. At last Miss Fawcett, who was herself trying to concentrate on a book, felt obliged to remark on her pupil's obvious lack of interest in her task.

The governess was not a strict authoritarian, nor an unfeeling woman. She was too shrewd not to realise that Anne's late uncle was unlamented as far as the girl was concerned; but she did allow for the present unsettling atmosphere of the household making it difficult for her charge to concentrate.

"I fear, Anne," she said, laying down her book, "that you are not making very much progress with your task."

Anne sighed. "No, Miss Fawcett — I'm so sorry." She was a biddable girl, who liked to please the governess, of whom she was quite fond. "But I don't seem able to give my mind to anything bookish this morning! Perhaps if I might have a breath of fresh air I should do better — it's so monstrously stuffy in the schoolroom, don't you think, ma'am? In spite of the windows being open."

The schoolroom was towards the top of the house, with small windows which did not admit much air on an exceptionally warm day such as this. Miss Fawcett agreed that this was so.

"Very well, my dear Anne, you may stroll about a little in the gardens. Return in, say, half an hour's time or so, and perhaps you will then feel ready for rational occupation."

Gratefully, Anne made her escape, scampering downstairs like a frisky rabbit and leaving the house unobtrusively by a side door. She skirted the formal gardens near to the house, choosing instead to walk in the shade of the trees which led down to the lake. She had almost reached the ornamental temple which stood beside it, when she saw another female figure about to mount the steps of the building. Recognising her mother's maid, Healey, Anne opened her lips to call a greeting; but something in the furtive look which Healey cast about her kept the girl silent. Instead, she drew back behind the shelter of a large, spreading oak, her slim form amply concealed. She watched with mounting curiosity.

Healey seemed satisfied that no one was about, for she wasted no more time in reconnaissance, but ran up the steps and disappeared into the temple. From where she was concealed, it was impossible for Anne to see into the building, which had only two small windows facing on to the steps. To approach nearer would be to risk discovery if Healey should suddenly emerge. Anne could not have explained why, but she felt instinctively that the maid was about some secret business, and would resent being spied upon. It might be no more than a meeting with some follower — did females as old as Healey have followers, the girl wondered? — but ever since the time when Anne had found Healey looking through her mother's correspondence, she had been suspicious of the maid. She decided to wait in hiding and see what transpired.

She had not long to wait. In about five minutes, Healey reappeared. This time, she did not look about her, but staggered down the steps like someone intoxicated. She was clutching something in her hand, but as she was facing away from Anne, the girl could not see what it was. She began to run with unsteady steps back towards the house. Once she stumbled and almost fell, but managed to right herself to continue her headlong flight.

For a while, Anne stared after her in amazement. Then, realising that Healey was unlikely to return, the girl ventured to approach the temple. She was cautious at first, fearing there might be someone within; but once she was close enough to peep through a window and see it was deserted, she entered quickly.

She looked about her. The temple was bare. She examined first the marble bench and then the floor, but could see nothing to indicate what Healey's errand could have been. Only a perverse curiosity made her stoop to look under the bench, for she had no genuine expectation of finding anything. After examining the area thoroughly, she presently gave an excited exclamation.

One of the floor tiles was loose, and a thin edge of paper protruded from beneath it.

With fingers that trembled slightly, Anne raised the tile to disclose a small piece of cheap, thin paper folded across.

She hesitated for a moment, glancing uneasily behind her.

No one was there. Hastily, she opened the note and read its brief contents, written in a hand obviously unaccustomed to literary exercise.

I'm scared theres a Bow Street man asking things I dont want no more leave me be for Gods sake.

Anne sat staring at the note for several minutes, uncertain what to do. Should she remove it and show it to someone in authority — her father, for instance? Or would it be better to replace it, but tell him about it? Anne, of course, knew nothing about the circumstances of her uncle's murder beyond what was common knowledge, and it was generally supposed that he had been killed by a burglar whom he had surprised in the act. That being so, she did not connect Healey's actions in any way with the murder. Nevertheless, the maid *had* been behaving strangely of late, and Anne felt that perhaps she ought to bring what she knew to someone's notice. The only thing was, to whose?

She started suddenly, fancying she heard a noise outside. She looked round apprehensively, but no one was there. The fright, short lived as it was, persuaded her to quit the temple and return to the safety of the schoolroom without further delay. Quickly she replaced the note in its hiding place, tucking it in more securely than Healey had done — for there could be no doubt that it was Healey who had left it there — and taking to her heels. She ran all the way back, pausing only to recover her breath a little before she climbed the stairs to the schoolroom. By then, she had decided whom she would tell: her bosom friend Fanny, recipient of all her secrets.

* * *

A few hours later that same day, Ross, one of the new grooms at Firsdale Hall, was sent into York on an errand to a saddler's. Having discharged this, he stabled his horse at a modest hostelry in the Shambles, then walked through into Coney Street. As he passed the great clock of St Martin le Grand overhanging the street, he paused for a moment to gaze up at the figure on top, the 'Little Admiral' holding his sextant. Then he crossed over to enter the Black Swan, one of York's coaching inns.

He was inside only a short time before emerging to walk down to the Mansion House, then turn right across St Helen's Square, and so into Stonegate. Just beyond the Olde Starre Inn a plaster figure of a red devil crouched beneath the eaves of a printer's establishment at the entrance to a narrow alley called Coffee Yard; advisedly so, since the buildings were chiefly coffee houses.

Ross entered one of these, finding a small, rather dark room with few customers. He made his way towards a bench at the far end, where a solitary man was sitting, his face in shadow. The two greeted each other casually, then put their heads together in earnest conversation.

Joe Watts, who had been keeping Ross under surveillance since the groom had left Firsdale Hall, went soft footed into the coffee house once he saw that the two men were absorbed in their talk. He beckoned to the proprietor, and unostentatiously displayed the short truncheon he carried in his pocket with the Crown stamp on its head, insignia of the Bow Street Runners.

"Yon man in the corner who's been joined by the newcomer," he said. "Know who he is?"

The proprietor shook his head, looking worried.

"Ever seen him before?" persisted Watts.

"Ay, a time or two. But what's amiss? Ye bain't after him, I hope, for this is a respectable house, and I don't want no fuss and botheration. How'm I to know what folks be up to? As long as they come in quiet and drink their coffee, I can't hardly be blamed for owt wrong, can I, now?"

Watts ignored this. "Does he meet other men here regular, like?"

The man considered. "Happen he does. Ay, now ye mention it, the once or twice I've noticed him, there's usually been some other cove who's come in to join him arterwards. But folk do meet here — that's the purpose o' a coffee house. Like a tavern, only not so noisy," he explained, with heavy sarcasm.

"And you can't say where he comes from?"

"No, I know nowt about him. He's not a regular, ye understand, like some. Just looks in now and then."

Watts nodded, cautioned the man to say nothing about the inquiry, and slipped quietly from the shop.

He returned to Stonegate, and crossed over into the Olde Starre Inn, where he was staying. A man loitering in the entrance hall approached him respectfully. This was a constable borrowed from the York contingent; one who, in Watts' opinion, most nearly approached the standard of a Cockney counterpart. Watts issued his orders, and the constable at once left the inn for Coffee Yard.

As for Watts, he went round to the stables to collect his horse for the short ride back to Firsdale. There might be no harm in a groom from Bradford meeting a friend in a York coffee house, but it would be as well to keep an eye open.

10

"I TOLD you that I should have been the one to interview the maid Healey, and not Runner Watts," said Anthea, accusingly. "I would not have been put off by what was most likely a feigned swoon."

"I doubt if she would have submitted to your questioning, in the first place. After all, you've no authority at all over her. Moreover, it would have been difficult to justify such a proceeding to de Ryde, would it not? Watts was the obvious, official interrogator."

Anthea agreed doubtfully to this.

The pair had been strolling around the paddock at the Knavesmire, where the Firsdale Hall party had been since noon on that same day. Justin had seized an opportunity when they were a little apart from the others, to give her an account of events earlier that morning.

Their isolation did not last, for they were soon joined again by Julia Marton,

Louisa and Rogers. Sir George, finding locomotion painful and difficult in all the crowd, had chosen to remain seated in the grandstand, where he had the company of several neighbours. Harry, as usual, had gone off with his young friends.

Justin groaned as he saw the Cholmondleys' party approaching, but there was no way of avoiding an exchange of greetings.

"Oh, my dear Lady Marton!" gushed Mrs Cholmondley. "Is it not the most melancholy thing that an outsider should win the last race? And there I had placed a substantial wager on the favourite! So, too, had my dear spouse, not to mention these other gentlemen — well, I think perhaps Mr Thrixen did not do so, nor Mr Barnet, but poor Sir John was 'in the suds', as the gentlemen say! Mr Reade, I forget — did you wager on Rising Sun, also?"

"Not I, ma'am!" laughed Reade. "To my mind, any filly with a name like that is bound to be a disappointment, what, Barnet? Notice you didn't risk y'r blunt on the nag."

"Not really a betting man," returned

the other, but without a trace of an apology. "That's to say, unless I can bet on a certainty."

"What an admission!" exclaimed Fulford, looking to Anthea for support. "I'm sure, Miss Rutherford, that you can't approve such a cautious fellow!"

"On the contrary," she answered, with a twinkle, "it's no bad thing for a gentleman to avoid deep doings in gambling and such like activities."

"Ah, but you, with your carefree nature, ma'am, must abhor these penny pinching notions! I see you as a lady of initiative and enterprise — pray do not disillusion me!"

He had moved closer to her as he spoke, looking up into her face with open admiration. Rogers, seeming to stumble, trod on his foot.

"Hell and — !" he broke off the imprecation with an effort. "I beg your pardon, Miss Rutherford, but I was taken unawares — I recommend you to look where you're going, sir!"

This, sharply, to Rogers, who apologised promptly. Justin studiously avoided his eye.

"I do trust that you will all look in on us whenever you feel inclined," said Mrs Cholmondley to Julia. "It was prodigiously pleasant, yesterday evening, don't you agree, Lady Marton? And there's no occasion for standing on ceremony with my dear Cholmondley and myself, as you must very well know by this time! Of all things, we welcome company! Pray don't wait upon a formal invitation, but just drop in upon us, any of your party."

Julia promised that she would, and issued a similar invitation in her turn.

"Well, what would you have me do?" she demanded, in answer to protests from Justin and Anthea when they had parted from the Cholmondleys. "Civility required no less, but I dare say they won't take us up on it. In any event, I must for very shame invite them to dine with us before long."

There were general groans at this threat as they moved back to the grandstand.

"I do believe," said Anthea to Rogers, "that you deliberately trod on Sir John Fulford's toes."

The two were walking quite by chance

a little apart from the others.

"What in the world can have given you that notion, I wonder?" he countered, with an attractive lop-sided grin.

She gave him a saucy look.

"For the life of me, I cannot imagine," she countered.

"No, indeed. Well, I must admit that I find that gentleman's gallantry towards you odious, and I cannot credit that you precisely relish it yourself?"

"Oh, but surely you realise, sir, that to a female all admiration is welcome? Poor creatures that we are, we need to be paid compliments and made pretty speeches to — what would we do without these tributes to our beauty and charm?"

"Now you think to roast me, ma'am. This may be true of some females, but I'll take my oath you're not one of such a paltry breed! How can you think to take me in with such stuff? But I know well that you don't, and I'm a fool to rise to the bait. The trouble is — " his voice took on a serious note — "I *am* a fool where you're concerned, Miss Anthea. And well you're aware of it!"

"I must say *that* remark is scarcely flattering!"

He looked at her, bewitching as she was, her hazel eyes glinting with mischief under a most becoming bonnet trimmed with lilac ribbons, and a few stray dark curls peeping from beneath it. He caught his breath, paused in his stride and almost — but not quite — seized her in his arms.

"Miss Anthea!" he said, in a voice not quite steady. "Surely you must know — "

At that moment, their tête-à-tête was abruptly interrupted by Harry, who arrived with two or three of his young friends, chattering away like starlings and effectively putting an end to all private conversation. Lady Marton announced that it was time they were getting back to poor George.

"For he'll be moped to death without us, you may depend! He finds it so frustrating not to be able to join us in strolling about between races."

Justin cocked a cynical eyebrow at Rogers, who managed to recover from his previous mood sufficiently to reply in kind. The interlude between his friend and Anthea had not passed unobserved by Justin, however, and he speculated upon how long it would be before Sprog declared himself. Also — and perhaps this was the more intriguing speculation — what answer that bewitching but undoubtedly flirtatious niece of his would make to the poor fellow. At present, she seemed unruffled.

"I must say, Aunt Julia, that Uncle George appeared tolerably content when we left him," laughed Anthea. "He and Mr Deering were disputing the points of one of the racehorses in most lively style!"

"Well, I'm sure I wish him joy of it, my dear Anthea, for truth to tell, I have had my fill of horseracing for today, and have more than a suspicion of the headache," replied Julia, forlornly. "However, I don't mean to spoil everyone's pleasure by saying I wish to go home."

Both young ladies commiserated with her; but by now the menfolk were chatting among themselves about the prospects for the next race, so paid no heed.

An idea suddenly came to Anthea.

"Aunt Julia, would you truly like to

return home?" she asked, solicitously. "If so, I'll willingly accompany you, for I, too, have seen sufficient racing for one day."

Julia Marton turned to her eagerly. "Oh, would you, indeed, my dear? But then — " her face fell — "we cannot leave poor Louisa without any female company. She'll find it so flat and dull with all the gentlemen of our party doing nothing but talking of horseflesh, and no doubt quite ignoring her."

Louisa, who had been hoping to see Mr Giles Crispin among the racegoers but had now quite given up any expectation of doing so, hastened to say that she would not mind at all if she left the Knavesmire before the final two races.

The decision to leave early was conveyed to Justin and Rogers, who dutifully attended the three ladies to the family carriage, and undertook to explain matters to Sir George, who could readily command a seat in one of the neighbours' carriages. Justin and Rogers had travelled to the Knavesmire in Justin's curricle.

If there was the slightest lingering over handing Anthea up into the carriage on the part of Rogers, the others studiously ignored it. In spite of her headache, Julia Marton reflected that perhaps her scheme was not going altogether awry, although she had nearly despaired of it.

* * *

Anthea was genuinely fond of her aunt, so her solicitude was not entirely feigned. Nevertheless, when the idea of returning home early was mooted, she had been struck all at once by a splendid notion. If she could be free for a while from Justin's keen eye, might she not find an opportunity to go alone to Denby House, and possibly enlist Anne de Ryde's help in gaining an interview with Healey?

Fortune was with her to an unexpected degree. Anne was in fact at Firsdale Hall with her governess in attendance, and closeted with Fanny Marton. The girl had been confiding to Fanny her experience earlier that same day with Healey, and they were both trying to decide what ought to be done. The appearance of Anthea seemed providential. Here was someone less awe-inspiring than a parent;

one of themselves, yet older and with more experience of the world.

As soon as Lady Marton had taken herself off to lie down, Fanny contrived to draw Louisa and Miss Fawcett out of the room for long enough to enable Anne to tell her story to Anthea.

"What do you think I should do, Miss Rutherford?" the girl concluded. "It may be only a private concern of Healey's — a follower, perhaps, though I should have supposed her to be too old for that! Yet the mention of the Bow Street Runner in her note, and then that other strange incident, when she was searching through Mama's correspondence some days since — Fanny told me she had repeated that confidence of mine to you, for she didn't wish me to think her underhand, and of course, I don't think any such thing, and indeed, was relieved that she should have done so, for now you can see that I had good reason to spy upon Healey, though in general I would think it a shabby thing to do — "

Anthea put a hand on her arm.

"Pray, my dear Anne, do pause for breath a moment!" she pleaded, smiling.

"There are one or two things I'd like to ask you. To begin with, when did this occur? I refer to your walk near the temple when you saw Healey."

"Oh, that was quite early on this morning — about eleven o'clock, I think, well before luncheon, at all event."

Anthea glanced at the clock.

"And it's now almost six hours later," she said, thoughtfully. "Do you know, Anne, I think it would be as well for me to see this note of Healey's? Perhaps we may contrive for Fanny and myself to walk back home with you, and to shake off Miss Fawcett once we are at Denby House, so that the three of us can visit that temple alone."

Like all girls of her age, Anne was intrigued at the thought of a conspiracy, and readily agreed. The affair turned out not too difficult to manage; Louisa decided not to accompany them to Denby House, and Miss Fawcett was intent upon a rest in her room before changing for dinner.

The three conspirators therefore set out for the temple in the grounds. As they approached it, some of the uneasiness which Anne had felt that morning once more came over her. She hung back, pulling at Anthea's arm, reluctant to leave the shelter of the trees.

Anthea looked at her a shade impatiently.

"What is it?"

"Hush! Not so loud," breathed Anne. "Suppose there should be someone inside — I'm scared!"

"Fustian!" exclaimed Anthea, in rallying tones. "We've nothing to fear in broad daylight, surely! I tell you what, though, Anne, if you don't care to enter, I'll go myself."

But this was quite against the code of honour of the two younger girls; whatever timorous feelings they might have, they could not bring themselves to allow a friend to 'stand buff', as Harry Harvey would have phrased it.

They at once shook their heads and bravely ranged themselves alongside her. Together they advanced towards the temple, paused a moment at the bottom of the short flight of steps, then entered, boldly.

No one was within.

After hesitating for a few moments, Anne went over to the place where she had found the loose tile, and stooped to raise it. The others crowded round eagerly.

"It's gone! There's nothing there now!"

She turned a face of deep disappointment towards them.

"Are you quite sure that was the place?" asked Anthea. "Could you not be mistaken?"

Anne refuted this indignantly, and Anthea was inclined to believe her. From what she had seen of the girl, Anne appeared to be a sensible, reliable young female, by no means as scatterbrained as many girls still in the schoolroom.

Nevertheless, they all set themselves to examining the tiles under the circular bench in search of another loose one.

"It's of no use," said Anne at last, squatting on her haunches in a way that would have horrified Miss Fawcett. "I knew all along that was the place! Someone has taken it away! Do you think — " her voice trembled a little — "do you think it was taken by the person it was intended for? If so, he may not be far away at the moment — oh, Miss Rutherford, what should we do?"

Anthea indicated that they should sit down on the bench.

"I'll try to advise you presently," she replied, calmly, "but first repeat to me that message, as nearly as possible word for word."

Learning by rote came high on Miss Fawcett's educational list, so Anne was able to oblige.

"She'd have written that to some man, don't you think, Miss Rutherford?" she asked, at the end. "It wouldn't have been a female, surely?"

"No, I'm confident it was a man. There's more in this affair than you know of, Anne — and it's better that you should *not* at present," she added quickly, seeing curiosity alive in the faces of both girls. "Oh, I know it's odious to be kept out of secrets, for I, too, have suffered in my turn! But until my Uncle Justin Rutherford and Watts, the Bow Street Runner have cleared up the dastardly business of your uncle's murder, we must all guard our tongues."

"Uncle Eustace's murder?" echoed

Anne, wide eyed, while Fanny, too, stared. "Do you mean to say that Healey's note has some bearing on *that*? But that must mean — "

She broke off, appalled at the thoughts leaping into her mind.

"Anne — Fanny — both of you!" Anthea's voice was stern, most unlike her usual tone. "I charge you *most solemnly* not to breathe a word of all this to a soul until you have permission from my Uncle Justin! Do you promise?"

Fanny nodded, obviously not a little frightened.

"But — but — Papa!" gulped Anne. "Surely he has a right to know if Healey is involved in anything so serious?"

"Don't worry, my dear, of course he will be told. But you can quite see that he won't wish *you* to know, can you not? So you must keep it all to yourself. And now, I want to talk to Healey. Can you arrange for me to see her somewhere privately, without anyone else in the household being aware of it?"

Anne looked doubtful.

"She's with Mama most of the time,

and Mama has been confined to her bed since Uncle Eustace was murdered. She sees no one, and Dr Clent gives her sedatives. Poor Mama, she's dreadfully distressed, for all that Uncle Eustace took advantage of her shamefully!"

Anthea nodded sympathetically. "Family affection takes no heed of a person's faults, mercifully for most of us. But is there no way you can think of?"

"Perhaps if you were to come up to the schoolroom," Anne said, brightening. "You can be quite private there, and at this time of day, none of the servants will be about. If I tell Healey that you require a few words with her, she won't dare refuse."

* * *

"You wished to see me, madam?"

Healey entered the schoolroom in response to Anthea's summons, closing the door behind her. She looked deathly pale and her hands were tightly clasped in front of her.

"Yes, Healey. Pray sit down. How is your mistress?"

The maid's lips trembled as she obeyed.

"Not at all well, madam, I'm sorry to say."

"You don't look at all well yourself," said Anthea, gently. "No doubt this dreadful business is playing upon your nerves, too."

The kind tone was too much for Healey. She burst into tears.

"Oh, ma'am, it do that — if only you knew — if only I could tell you — "

The words were punctuated by sobs. Anthea rose, putting a comforting arm briefly around the maid's shoulders.

"There, there. But I *do* know, Healey."

The sobbing checked abruptly as Healey raised a tear stained face to Anthea's.

"You *do*, ma'am? But how can you possibly?"

Anthea resumed her seat.

"No matter how," she said calmly, "but, believe me, I am fully informed about events from the long distant past which have a bearing on Sir Eustace Knowle's murder. I've also been told what was said in the interview between you and the Bow Street Runner Watts earlier today. It seems, Healey, that there was one question you failed to answer.

"I — I — I feel queer, ma'am — I'm going to swoon — "

The maid swayed in her chair, but Anthea leapt forward and forced her head down between her knees.

"I dare say," she said, ruthlessly, "And I'm sure you've sufficient reason. But you are the only person who can give any guidance to the identity of Sir Eustace's murderer, and you *must* speak. Otherwise there may be yet more murders — do you understand?"

Healey moaned, but sat upright, supporting her face in her hands. Anthea stood back from her, waiting. It was several moments before the maid spoke.

"All right, I'll tell. But that Runner'll need to keep an eye on me, for Gawd only knows what'll become of me, else! He's a fiend in human shape! Yes, I did see him."

Anthea felt a surge of excitement, but she schooled herself to listen patiently and ask all the important questions.

At the conclusion of Healey's account,

however, she had to admit to herself that she was disappointed. Apart from confirming that the ex-convict was in the neighbourhood, Healey could offer no positive help in identifying him.

"Is there nothing?" Anthea pressed her desperately. "You say his face was masked and he wore a cloak, so I can quite see that would be a sufficient disguise for one whom you hadn't seen for close on fifteen years, especially as it was dark in the temple. But was there no mannerism — a trick of gesture or something of that kind — familiar to you from the past? It's often by such small things that we truly recognise people."

"Now that you mention it," replied the maid, thoughtfully, "there was — I don't know — something in his voice. It had altered, I can't tell how, maybe a trick of speaking in them outlandish parts where he'd been, but all the same, underneath I knew it, right enough."

"Famous!" exclaimed Anthea, enthusiastically. "I don't quite know how this can be turned to advantage, but — "

She was interrupted abruptly by the door being pushed open roughly so that it slammed against the wall. Anne erupted into the room with a wild expression on her face.

"You must come!" she shouted at Anthea, incoherently. "Pray come at once! Papa — we don't know — oh, please God, he may not die! Dr Clent's with him — you're needed, Healey — come, come quickly!"

11

IT was close on dinner time when Anthea and Fanny returned to Firsdale Hall. The gentlemen of the party were already indulging in a pre-prandial glass of sherry; Julia and Louisa were expected downstairs at any moment.

"Where the deuce have you been until now?" demanded Justin. "We'd best send a message to the kitchen, George, for if I know anything, it will take these two at least an hour to get into evening rig."

"Justin, never mind that," said Anthea, impatiently. "I must speak to you for a few moments alone. Fanny, you go and dress as expeditiously as possible, and tell my maid to lay out — oh, anything!"

Seeing the expression on her face, Justin at once took her arm and guided her into an ante-room. Sir George looked after them thoughtfully, but made no move to follow, having regard to his other guests. Whatever it was, no doubt he would learn about it in time.

"What's amiss?" asked Justin, when he had closed the door upon them. "Something at de Ryde's, I collect?"

She nodded. "Justin, I don't know where to begin! I went to Denby House thinking to see Healey — Anne was here, you see, when we returned from the Knavesmire, so it was quite natural that Fanny and I should walk back with her — "

"Did you speak with Healey?"

"How you do take one up! Yes, and very much to the purpose! Justin, she has seen this man, and is frightened to death of him!"

"Is she able to identify him?" asked Justin, getting to the point at once.

"Yes — no — that is to say, only by his voice. For the rest, she saw him only once, and then it was by night and in disguise."

She explained quickly about the meeting in the temple and the arrangements for messages, then went on to tell of the message found by Anne.

"And it had *gone*, Justin, by the time we reached the place about five o'clock, almost six hours later! That was before I went indoors to speak to Healey — and I never had an opportunity to ask her about that, for the most frightful thing occurred to interrupt us! Mr de Ryde had an accident in his curricle — the wheel came off and he was thrown to the ground!"

"Is he alive?" asked Justin, quickly.

"Yes, thank Heavens, but he's badly hurt. Concussed, says Dr Clent, with broken bones in his left leg and arm that will take some time to mend. It was fortunate that the doctor was in the house and could go to him at once. But, you know, Justin, it was no true accident, was it? It's just the same as Uncle George's — it was meant to kill, wasn't it? Because of those monstrous threatening letters!"

"I fear so. Do you know if any of the stable hands have examined the curricle? If not, I must put Watts on to the business at once — in any event, I'll send a message for him to the village inn. He's quartered there at present."

"I'm afraid I don't know, Justin — everything was in such confusion, as you may well imagine! Poor Anne — it's melancholy for her, with both her parents laid low! Dr Clent sent at once for her old nurse, who lives in a cottage in the village, to assist with the invalids, and he's also despatched a message to Anne's Aunt de Ryde, whom Anne likes amazingly considering she's a confirmed old maid. She'll take charge of the household very capably, I collect. Then, of course, Aunt Julia and Fanny will do all they can to support Anne, I know."

Justin nodded. "I see the medico has it all arranged admirably. Well, I'm relieved you told me this privately, though naturally I'll have to inform George and the others of de Ryde's accident. Don't forget, Anthea, that the females of our party as yet know of no connection between the murder and these other mishaps — no mention has been made of threatening letters, even between George and Julia. So the accident to de Ryde remains simply an accident, for the present."

"Yes, yes, I'll hold my tongue," she promised. "And now I *must* make haste, Justin!"

They parted, she to her bedroom to change her dress and he to dash off a brief note for Watts requesting his presence immediately.

When he returned to the parlour, Julia and Louisa were there, the latter looking delightfully demure in a white muslin gown trimmed with pink ruching at neck and hem.

"But where in the world are Anthea and Fanny?" demanded Julia, petulantly. "The gong struck these few minutes since! Really, it is a deal too bad — "

"Calm yourself, sister," said Justin. "They'll be here in a few minutes, and it's not entirely their fault that they're a trifle late."

He explained the situation in his most matter of fact tones. Julia and Louisa expressed real concern; Harry said it was a wretched business, then moved over to take another glass of sherry; while Sir George and Rogers looked sharply at their informant.

"What the devil's all this, eh?" asked Sir George presently, edging close to Justin and speaking *sotto voce*. "This accident anything like mine? You said de Ryde had received one of those damned letters."

Rogers, too, closed in on him, effectively shutting out the others from overhearing.

"Looks very much like it," replied Justin, quietly. "I've sent for Watts to go there — I'll join him myself as soon as dinner's over. There's more, but I can't tell you now."

"Perhaps over the wine after we've dined," suggested Sir George. "Though that young chap Harry ain't in the secret so far. Still, dare say he'll be discreet."

"No, sorry, I'm not staying — must get over to Denby House. And I think better not say anything to Harry, by the way."

"Not staying to drink a post-prandial glass?" repeated his brother-in-law, shocked. "Well, if that don't beat all! But I suppose you're right, and this business comes first. Glad it's not my pigeon, that's all, with the Runner here — not to mention you."

* * *

"What art doin' 'ere, do tha reckon?" demanded a groom truculently, planting himself squarely in the way of Joseph Watts when the Runner presented himself at the Denby House stables.

"Minding the King's business," Watts replied shortly, displaying the Crown stamp on his Runner's baton. "Where's your boss, cully?"

The groom's face changed and he stepped back.

"I'll fetch' im," he volunteered, running towards the tack room.

A moment later he was back with a square built Yorkshireman whose keen eyes belied the fleshy face and unhurried manner.

"I'm Webster, head groom," he announced. "Owt I can do for thee?"

Watts nodded. "I'm looking into the matter of Mr de Ryde's accident. Anything ye can tell me? How did it occur?"

"H'm, Bow Street Runner business, is it? Not surprised. Well, a wheel came off master's curricle as he was bowlin' down t'drive at a fair old rate. Vehicle tilted, of course, an' he was tipped out. By God's mercy, t'horses didn't trample 'im, though they was fair crazed, poor beasts. Master's bad enough, though, as doctor'll tell 'ee."

"I've seen the medico. Why aren't ye surprised that it's police business?"

"Got my reasons. That wheel, now. Took a good look, course, for anything in the way of negligence I won't bear with, sithee? Send the cove packin', that I would an' no mistake. All our vehicles is examined regular, as tha might know — I've been in t'stables man and boy these thirty an' more years. But t'axle that broke, sithee, that weren't no accident, nor yet no negligence, neither. Been proper messed about with, I'll tak' me oath on't! Part sawn through, ready to give way any minute — which it did."

Watts emitted a low whistle. "Ye've kept the evidence?"

"Ay, reckon I thought it'd be needed. But tha can't blame any o' my lads," he went on, defensively. "I can vouch for every last one, sithee! Been here most o' their lives, older lads, an' young 'uns more'n a few years — every man Jack on 'em keen on t'job, and not so daft as to do owt to lose it! Why should they, tell me that? Good places b'ain't so easy to come by, think on."

"Right enough. But what about an outsider? Someone breaking in after dark, for instance."

"Happen it's possible," said Webster, doubtfully. "But I reckon he'd be heard by t'lads who sleep in t'loft."

"When did Mr de Ryde have the curricle out last?"

"Tuesday," was the prompt reply. "Drove Sir Eustace to t'Kavesmire — ee, that was a bad business an' no mistake."

"The murder? Ay, it was indeed. So the vehicle was all right and tight two days since, eh? Anyone else lookin' it over since — one of the grooms, for instance?"

Webster shook his head. "Usually it'd be cleaned early t'next morning, ready for use. But what with t'poor gennelman bein' done in and found by t'gardener's lad, things was all anyhow, think on. No one went nigh it, not till maister came isself to t'stables this morning for it. B'ain't right, neither." He shook his head. "Always sends for t'curricle to be brought up to t'house. Was in a hurry, seemingly."

"Has anyone else been here during the

past two days, other than the regular stable staff? Here in the stables, I mean?"

Webster shook his head. "Not to t'stables. Plenty of folk came to t'house, thee was one, as tha knows." He paused a moment, then went on, "Come to think on't, though, there was a lad from Firsdale Hall called in wi' a message from Sir George this arternoon."

"What time?"

"'Bout four, I reckon."

"One of the grooms, eh? Which one?"

"Can't rightly say — one o' t'new lads." He raised his voice. "Here, Jem — which o' t'stable lads from Firsdale came here a while back?"

One of the grooms left off polishing a piece of tack and came forward, touching his cap respectfully to Watts.

"Ross, 'is name is, maister."

Watt's eye kindled. "Oh, yes? How long did he stay here, and exactly where did he go?"

The double question seemed too much for the groom's intelligence. He looked doubtfully at his superior, who explained it, and related the answers.

"Seems he was here nobbut half an

hour, Mr Watts. Went up to t'house to deliver his note, then come back to have another word wi' this lad, friendly like. They tak' a mug of ale together wi' some o' t'others in t'Black Horse now and then."

"Not close friends, then — drinking companions?" summed up Watts. "Listen to me, cully, and answer me carefully. Did Ross spend any time alone in the coach house where Mr de Ryde's curricle is kept? Did you leave him there for any reason? Think *hard* now — it's only a few hours agone."

The groom scratched his head, evidently giving the matter some thought, then produced a decided negative. Watts, disappointed, pressed him again, but received the same reply. It seemed that the two men were standing outside on the yard during their time together. This was confirmed by others.

"I take it he walked here?" asked Watts, at the end. "Wouldn't have needed a horse for that distance."

"Not he!" Webster guffawed. "Only tak's less than twenty minutes if tha goes gentry road — down both carriage drives.

But we allus uses back road — up t'lane past our stable, sithee, till tha comes to t'boundary wall o' t'Hall. There's a door no one but t'gardeners and stable lads mak' use on, hard by their stables. Ten minutes'd do it easy."

"I've a mind to try it myself. I'm due back at the Hall. Well, thankee, Webster, for your assistance. Good evening to ye."

He found the way without difficulty, meeting no one, and headed for the kitchens, where already he was sure of a favourable reception. Cook had taken to him at once, while the maids cast sheep's eyes in his direction whenever they could do so without calling down a reprimand upon their heads from their superiors. Even Oldroyd, the stately butler, pronounced him to be a very tolerable kind of man for a Bow Street Runner, a statement agreed by the footmen. There was no difficulty about accommodating him for dinner with them in the servants' hall; in the meantime, if Mr Watts could fancy a tankard of home brewed, he was very welcome. Mr Watts could, and accepted gratefully.

While imbibing this beverage, he conveyed a message upstairs to Justin by way of a footman, who soon returned with the reply that Watts should go up to the library. This he did, and was joined there in a few minutes by Justin, who had hastily excused himself from the dinner table when the final course had been reached.

Watts soon put him in possession of the latest news.

"I put a constable on to watch Ross, guv'nor, when I left York myself. Seems he didn't stay there long afterwards, since he was back here and visiting the Denby House stables at four o'clock. I'll hear exactly what he did when I get the man's report tomorrow — the constable wouldn't go outside the city bounds, of course, to follow him back here."

Justin nodded absently, rumpling his dark hair in the way he had when he was puzzling his way through a problem.

"It's possible this groom Ross may be our man, Joe — he's the right age, and fits the description we've got, such as it is. But several points don't coincide. Take my brother-in-law's accident, which is where the affair began, as we see now. We've already considered Ross as the culprit, and it won't fadge. Next, the meeting with Healey in the temple on the night of the masquerade. Possible. Carr says Ross wasn't on duty that evening, so he could have gone to Denby House, especially since you tell me there's a quicker and more secluded route. Healey gave the time at about nine o'clock, and staff wouldn't be active at that hour, so he'd be reasonably sure of not being observed. But then we come to de Ryde's accident, and there's no certainty about that, judging by the evidence. He was in the right place at the right time, but had no opportunity to tamper with the curricle."

"Reckon he's up to no good, all the same, sir, and if it's not murder, what is it? His movements are suspicious, to say the least. And couldn't he have got into the stables after dark to tamper with that axle? Most outdoor staff bed down for the night early, and I dare swear they sleep like hogs."

"As you say, Joe, it might have happened like that. But so far, we've only one incident out of three where his complicity is completely possible, and no positive evidence whatsoever. I think we must extend our horizons a little farther to consider every newcomer to the neighbourhood. We will need to examine their origins to ascertain that each of them has an established background. It will be a delicate business, but I'm positive it's the only way to flush out our quarry. Another useful move would be to question some of the servants — and perhaps the villagers — as to whether they've observed anything unusual at the times relevant to our inquiry. Let's start work on it now by drawing up a list."

* * *

"You know," said Anthea in a low tone to Justin, when he joined the family party later in the evening over the usual tea drinking. "There's one sure means of discovering whether or not that groom is the murderer, and that is to introduce him in some way to Healey! She said she could identify the man by his voice."

Justin nodded. True to his promise,

he had been keeping her informed of developments.

"Don't think we've overlooked that fact, Watts and I, my perspicacious niece," he answered, with one of his quizzical grins. "But a confrontation won't be too easy to arrange — I rather suppose that the maid will fight shy of it, for she's scared to death of the rogue. We're hoping to fix matters so that she's not obliged to come face to face with him, but to be in a position to overhear his voice. It may take a little time, therefore. Were we more convinced by the scanty evidence we possess, we should of course crowd on all sail, in the words of the navy. But I believe we can't afford to overlook other possibilities by pursuing Ross too hotly."

He paused to lay down the cup from which he had been drinking, shaking his head to Julia's offers of replenishment.

"One is quite enough, my dear sister. I'm persuaded that too much tea drinking can lead to developing a metallic lining in one's interior."

Julia opened her eyes wide. "No, truly, Justin? Did you get that advice from one of your smart London doctors?"

George Marton laughed outright, while the others smiled, not caring to bait their hostess.

"Don't know any — don't need to, I'm glad to say. But, Julia, my love," he continued in a wheedling tone, "there is something I'd like you to do for me tomorrow, something far more important than may appear. George will support me in this, I know."

He glanced at his brother-in-law, his eyes charged with meaning. Sir George interpreted the glance as intending an explanation later. He nodded.

"What is it?" asked Julia, suspiciously. "I know when you take that tone to me, Justin, you wish me to do something I've no desire to perform!"

"You may think that at first, but George will persuade you otherwise, you'll see. I want you to call upon Mrs Cholmondley and invite her and her party to join us in a day's pleasure excursion."

12

"MY dear Lady Marton, so kind of you to call — so obliging!" gushed Lady Cholmondley, as the Firsdale Hall ladies, accompanied by the Honourable Justin Rutherford and Mr Rogers were ushered into the morning parlour. "I was hoping you might take me up on my invitation to drop in upon us at any time! I said to Sir John and Mr Barnet — did I not, gentlemen?" she glanced for corroboration at these two, who had been seated beside her husband in the window " — that it would be so vastly enjoyable to have some of the neighbours calling today, since yesterday was the last day of the Races, you know, and we shall find ourselves quite desolate without something pleasurable to occupy ourselves — for my dear spouse has managed to prevail upon all our guests, excepting only Mr and Mrs Thrixen, whom we see frequently, you know — all our guests, as I say, have agreed to remain with us for a further period, so we shall be quite a merry party! I do think, do not you, Miss Rutherford, that nothing can be so pleasant as company when one lives in the depths of the country?"

Anthea gave her hostess a quizzical look.

"Not quite in the depths, ma'am, would you say? You are but a few miles from York, which anyone must allow is a considerable town."

"Oh, yes, of course you are in the right of it, but even a few miles tend to isolate one from the hurly-burly of town life. We are vastly dependent upon our neighbours, you know. Fortunately, we have such pleasant neighbours, and you might not believe, coming from London as you do, that here we dine regularly with more than twenty families! But so it is, is it not, James, my love?"

Mr James Cholmondley, thus appealed to, could not do other than give a brief assent, but he was still occupied in greeting his visitors, having risen from his chair as soon as they entered. The other men had come to their feet, too, and now a general bustle arose until everyone was seated again.

With his usual adroitness, Sir John Fulford had managed to secure a seat next to Louisa and Anthea, who had the plump, genial Mr Fellowes on their other side. Justin had deliberately seated himself so that he could converse easily with Cholmondley's two other guests, Mr Barnet and Mr Reade, while Rogers was beside the host.

"You have the reputation of being prodigiously hospitable, Mrs Cholmondley," said Julia, partly in response to the last remark.

"But then I've always been told that Yorkshire hospitality is famed," said Anthea. "Do you all reside in the county? If so, modesty will prevent you from agreeing with the dictum."

She looked around at the assembled company with a challenging smile. Justin repressed a frown, fearing that perhaps, in his own phrase, she was doing it too brown.

"That's assuming, ma'am, that we any of us possess that virtue," replied Barnet, with an answering smile. "I don't think it likely, do you, Fulford?"

"Speak for yourself," retorted the other. "But I believe, ma'am, that Fellowes here is the only Yorkshireman among the four of us. I trust it don't place him too high in your favour — I assure you that just as good men come from other parts."

"Assuredly," replied Anthea, trying to ignore the ogling which accompanied this remark. "What part of the county do you reside in, Mr Fellowes?"

"Not far from Whitby, Miss Rutherford — the north Yorkshire moors, you know. Very salubrious, dear lady, indeed. A sad pity that it's too far for you to visit on a day's outing from here. But perhaps at some time, if your parents should ever be in that way — I collect that they are visiting the Lakes at present?"

Anthea answered that indeed they were, and a lively discussion on the beauties of the Lake District followed, in which everyone joined.

"Speaking of outings," said Julia, responding to a sideways glance from her brother, "some of our young people are considering a day's excursion to Helmsley, to see the castle, you know, and then go on to visit Rievaulx Abbey.

They wondered if perhaps any of your guests would care to join them? You and your husband must often have been to Helmsley, as indeed so have Sir George and myself, but we have never yet visited Rievaulx Abbey. It is owned by the Duncombes, you know, and they have given permission to view it."

Fulford at once declared it a splendid notion, and demanded that the other three men should support him. Justin noticed that their response, though civil, was somewhat lacking in enthusiasm. Nevertheless, he thought that he could count on all of them, if only because it was difficult to back out without infringing the accepted code of polite behaviour. And he particularly wished for all of them to be present.

"Well, we shall go too, shall we not, my dear?" Mrs Cholmondley said to her husband. "Yes, of course we've been to Helmsley many times, but what of that? An excursion with a congenial party of friends is always a vastly pleasurable affair! And a visit to Rievaulx Abbey — that is something, indeed! Do you mean to go, Lady Marton? And Sir George also?"

"My husband begs to be excused, since travelling and sightseeing are a penance to him at present. I thought I might go, however, as chaperone, for my younger daughter Fanny will be quite wild to go, I know. And perhaps we might see if poor little Anne de Ryde would be permitted by her mama to make one of the party, for although she is in mourning, it will be hard if a child in the schoolroom may not have an occasional outing in a discreet kind of way. I don't know," she added, as Mrs Cholmondley hastened to express agreement with this, "if you've heard the latest melancholy news from Denby House?"

"News from Denby House?" demanded Cholmondley quickly. "What's this, ma'am?"

The company had been chatting together in a desultory way about the proposed outing; but now a silence fell, as their attention was caught.

"Yes," echoed his wife, "what can you mean, Lady Marton? Surely not — not another disaster? Oh, no, pray do not say so!"

Justin surreptitiously studied the faces of Cholmondley's four guests as Julia answered.

"I fear it's very bad. Mr de Ryde had an accident in his curricle yesterday evening, and — "

"Not killed!" exclaimed Mrs Cholmondley, in great distress. "No, not — not that!"

"No, ma'am," put in Justin quickly. "It is not so bad as that, mercifully. He's suffered a concussion and several broken bones, but there's no fear for his life."

It seemed to Justin that both Reade and Barnet had been holding their breath until he spoke. Now they let out deep sighs — of relief, he wondered?

"Thank God for that!" said Cholmondley, fervently. "But how did it occur? Where? Was it a collision?"

Fulford and Fellowes echoed these queries almost in the same breath. They, too, had been listening with strained attention.

"Pray ring for the servant, James," implored Mrs Cholmondley, for once in failing accents. "I need my vinaigrette — I feel quite faint!"

Julia produced the required article from her reticule, and passed it over to her hostess.

"I'm so sorry, my dear Mrs Cholmondley — I didn't mean to inflict such a shock upon you. I quite thought you might have already heard."

"Some of us were out riding earlier this morning," said James Cholmondley, "but we didn't go near the village, which is where one learns everything. And, for once, the servants don't seem to be in the know — that is unusual, I grant you! The servants' hall is a hotbed of gossip!"

"And why not?" asked Barnet, with an ironical smile. "What else is there to entertain them but the affairs of their betters?"

"Lucrative, too, on occasion," added Fulford. "Quite a bit of hush money must change hands in most households."

"I'm sure you would know about that," put in Reade, giving him a sly glance.

"Gentlemen, pray don't jest about such a serious matter!" implored Mrs Cholmondley. "We can only be thankful that poor Mr de Ryde is not more seriously injured, and especially since the dreadful affair of his brother-in-law's murder! Poor, dear Mary de Ryde will be in a melancholy way — already she has taken to her bed, and Dr Clent is in constant attendance! I must send round a sympathetic message — for, of course, it's out of the question that she will wish to see anyone at present, though I shall say that if there's anything at all I can do — "

Her husband echoed these neighbourly sentiments, and Julia explained what measures had been taken by the doctor to ensure the comfort of the household. Both Mr and Mrs Cholmondley expressed their relief at this, for they were undeniably good-hearted people.

"But you haven't told us precisely what occurred," complained Fellowes.

Justin and his friend Rogers exchanged a brief, warning glance.

"It seems a wheel came off de Ryde's curricle as he was setting out down the drive at Denby House," said Justin. "The vehicle overturned, of course, and he was thrown heavily to the ground."

"A wheel came off!" exclaimed Reade. "What kind of stable does the fellow keep, in God's name? Don't he have his vehicles properly cared for?"

"Naturally, in the normal course. But one must remember that there's been a deal of commotion there of late, and routine may have been allowed to lapse a trifle."

"Has anyone had a word with the head groom?" asked Cholmondley. "I don't know quite whose business it would be to do so, but I feel very strongly that such criminal negligence should not go unreproved! What has Sir George to say about it, Rutherford?"

Justin silently cursed the direct question, which he could see no way of avoiding. He had been trying to play down the accident as much as possible, in the hope that one of those present — among whom he thought there was a strong probability that the murderer might be found — should reveal himself by betraying some inside knowledge. Cholmondley, in his usual voluble fashion, had more or less disposed of that hope. However, Justin's quick mind foresaw that the visit of Watts to de Ryde's stables would soon be a matter of local gossip, do what he might to prevent it; so he bowed to the inevitable.

"He's naturally very concerned, and would have gone round at once when we heard the news yesterday evening, but for his injury. However, he sent Watts, the Bow Street Runner, to look into the business and try to ascertain if any of the stable hands had been negligent."

"Did he discover anything?" asked Barnet.

It seemed to Justin that the eyes of all four of Cholmondley's guests were fixed on him with intensity. Was there one of them, he wondered, who knew more of this matter than he himself did? When he replied, it was in a casual tone tinged with regret.

"He was told more or less what I've just repeated to you — that the murder had so disorganised the normal working routine as to make the grooms forgetful of certain of their duties. Examining all the vehicles in the coach house would, of course, have been one of these."

"Yes, but — " began Barnet.

"But what precisely was *wrong* with the wheel?" interrupted Fulford and Reade, more or less in chorus.

"What caused it to come off?" supplemented Fellowes. "Did the linch pin break? One does prefer to know, so as to be sure to take proper care oneself."

Justin nodded. "That, and it seems there was also a weakness in the axle."

"Well, it sounds a devilish odd thing to happen in a well-run gentleman's stable!" exclaimed Reade. "If it were mine, I'd sack the lot of 'em, I can tell you!"

There was a chorus of agreement with this.

"But possibly the curricle was one that had been too long on the road," put in Barnet.

"Shouldn't think that likely," retorted Cholmondley. "Not with de Ryde. Drives bang-up equipages — quite noted for it in the neighbourhood, I assure you."

To Justin's relief, their hostess turned the subject.

"I beg you won't say any more!" she pleaded, in a faint voice. "I declare I am quite overcome, as it is. I must write a note to Mary de Ryde at once."

Julia rose to her feet.

"Perhaps we should take our leave now, Mrs Cholmondley. I dare say you may prefer not to undertake the outing to Helmsley at the present time. I shall quite understand."

"Oh, no," replied that lady, rallying quickly. "If we could help our neighbours in any way by giving up the scheme, of course we would. But it seems a pity to deprive our guests, yours and mine, of such a pleasurable outing — such a vastly good notion of yours, Lady Marton! I am sure they are all looking forward to it prodigiously, so we cannot disappoint them, can we? Do let us make our arrangements for it now, while you are here — that is, if you can spare a little longer?"

Her husband echoed this enthusiastically; so after some discussion, Tuesday of the following week was appointed and suitable transport for everyone arranged.

* * *

"Seems to me," said Justin, "that only Fulford was keen on the scheme. The other three would have refused if they could have done the thing civilly."

"And *he* only wishes to join the party so that he can flirt with Miss Anthea!" exclaimed Rogers, disgustedly. "A loose fish, if ever I met one!"

"Still, it may give Anthea the chance to find out something about him — where he comes from, how long he's been there, and so on," Justin answered, reflectively. "It's devilish tricky knowing quite how to tackle the business of obtaining information about these people."

"I must say, old chap, that I don't entirely agree with the notion of your niece having to put up with that oaf's amorous overtures simply to assist your investigation," retorted Rogers, with some heat. "Damned if I do!"

"Oh, Anthea's perfectly able to take care of herself."

Sir George, who had been listening to the two friends giving an account of their morning call, ignored all this and went straight to the point.

"I collect that you think it unwise to attempt the straightforward tactic of asking Cholmondley to supply information about his guests?"

Justin nodded. "I might try a casual question or so. Difficulty is, I'd have to tell him the whole story in order to question him outright and we've agreed at this stage, anyway, that's inadvisable. He's a good chap, but such a gossip monger, that there's no hope of relying on his discretion."

"That's true. And we don't wish to alarm the whole neighbourhood by informing them that there's a murderer in their midst, even though we're confident that the felon means mischief only to those of us who were concerned in that bygone affair," agreed Sir George. "At present, the general opinion is that Knowle was murdered by a burglar whom he caught in the act. Better keep it like that for as long as possible."

"Indeed, far better. It gives us a stronger chance, too, of uncovering the culprit. What Joe Watts and I have decided is that we'll investigate every newcomer to the district between us. At the moment, he's taking the few candidates there are among servants and villagers — certainly not many — and also questioning local people about comings and goings relevant to the crimes. My part is with newcomers among the gentry, and requires a more oblique approach, as you'll appreciate."

"That's why you thought this excursion to Rievaulx Abbey might be of service — bring some of these suspects under surveillance, so to speak?" asked Sir George.

"That, and attempting to get on the kind of easy terms with them when they'll chat to us, tell us something about themselves."

"You realise, of course, that if the guilty man *is* among them, he won't divulge anything of significance?"

"Yes, but one of the others may — or even he may let drop a hint unawares." Justin shrugged. "I'm not an ardent gambling man, but I must risk a hazard now and then. However, I must confess I could think of no quicker way of insinuating myself — and my attendant spies — " with a grin at Rogers, who looked a trifle unresponsive — "among the enemy. Julia has indicated that her troubled social conscience will drive her to invite them to dine before long, but I couldn't wait for that."

"The rest of us, however," said Sir George, glumly, "can manage to wait for it tolerably well, assure you! A good chap, Cholmondley, and his wife the best of women, no doubt, but — "

Rogers and Justin laughed.

"I must remember to thank my sister, by the by, for her co-operation in the matter of the outing," remarked Justin. "She certainly turned up trumps."

"Yes, but I fear there may be a reckoning," warned Sir George. "Julia ain't the hen witted female you may fancy her — that's a fault of brothers — and God knows what I'm to tell her if she starts asking questions again! She did yesterday evening after you'd asked her to invite the Cholmondleys on that outing, but I managed to fob her off then. Next time she pesters me, I shall send her straight to you, and so I warn you!"

His fears were justified, for no sooner was luncheon over, than his wife stalked into the library where he was half dozing over a book. She had the air of a woman who means business.

"What *is* all this nonsense, George?" she demanded, sitting down with a flourish. "Don't tell me there's not something vastly odd going on between you and that unregenerate younger brother of mine, for I shan't believe you! Why was it so important to him that I should invite the Cholmondleys on an expedition to Helmsley and Rievaulx Abbey?"

"Didn't need to be Helmsley in particular," replied her spouse, carelessly.

"Don't prevaricate! Why is Justin going out of his way to seek their company? If they had a nubile daughter," she added, with a sly smile, "I could understand it, of course, but the entire household — except for Maria Cholmondley, and I cannot suppose him so lost to all natural taste as to nourish a passion for *her* in his bosom! — as I say, the entire household is male. And not, I would have thought, the kind of people to have anything in common with my brother, even allowing for his sporting proclivities as well as his academic interests."

Sir George hesitated, then appeared to make up his mind.

"No, you're in the right of it, m'dear. Your brother don't care a rush for any of Cholmondley's guests. He needs to seek their company for quite another reason."

She registered alarm. "Don't tell me, George, that he's becoming involved in one of those unsavoury mystery investigations that our elder brother Edward was telling us of, while he was here! I cannot imagine — but, yes, of course, I see it all, now! The murder of Sir Eustace Knowle — that Runner from Bow Street who's always haunting Justin's footsteps — " She broke off, frowning.

"George," she demanded, presently. "Tell me *truly*, now — the whole neighbourhood believes that Knowle was killed by an intruder whom he surprised; but *is that so*? You as a JP will naturally know more about this than others. Does Justin suspect some other murderer, and moreover one who is in our midst? If so, I think it only right and proper that you should tell me. Believe me, I know how to be discreet, and can act a part as well as the next female! But I must know what is going on."

13

AFTER the Firsdale Hall party had left Warton Manor, Mrs Cholmondley bustled out of the room to arrange some domestic matters with her staff, while the gentlemen remained chatting together for a while.

"Now you must allow that we have eminently pleasant neighbours!" exclaimed Cholmondley, enthusiastically. "Only think, for them to take the trouble to invite us to join them in a day's outing, and it's not even as if they were particularly acquainted with you four gentlemen! But I take it as being out of compliment to Mrs Cholmondley and myself — Sir George and his good lady are never lacking in those little attentions which mean so much among neighbours."

"You are indeed fortunate, Cholmondley," agreed Fellowes. "I am somewhat isolated from my neighbours at home, you know, but then I travel about a good deal."

"Where do your travels take you?" asked Barnet, in a casual tone.

"Oh, London, Brighton, and to racecourses up and down the country — wherever the spirit moves me to go. I'm by way of being a wanderer. I'll be off to Doncaster for the St Leger next month."

"I might join you," said Reade impulsively. Then, trying to weaken the implied invitation, "That's to say, if circumstances permit, I'll be there. Dare say the rest of you fellows will, too? Sure to run across each other."

He could think of few things more boring than another dose of Fellowes's company, a dull stick if ever he met one, so he hastened to change the subject.

"Odd thing about that chap de Ryde's accident," he continued. "Some negligence somewhere, I'll take my oath. Heads would roll, believe me if it occurred to any vehicle of mine!"

"So you indicated earlier," remarked Barnet. "That fellow Rutherford seemed to be playing the business down, no doubt in deference to the tender feelings of our hostess. I'd hazard a guess that he could have told us more."

"Perhaps so, for he is Marton's brother-in-law, after all," said Cholmondley, "and as a Justice of the Peace, Sir George hears of anything untoward hereabouts. Well, Reade, you must admit that any negligence will certainly be discovered with no less an investigator than a Bow Street Runner looking into the affair."

"The Runner was originally sent up to York for the Lord Mayor's ball, wasn't he?" demanded Fulford. "Because of some jewel robberies in the district?"

Cholmondley nodded. "Quite an outbreak of them, you know, both in the town itself and in some outlying parts. The Hartes at Strensall and the Terrys at Flaxton, not more than six or seven miles from here, were burgled recently, and the felons never found. Nor the valuables, which one does hope for. As I expect you know, receivers of stolen goods often advertise, offering to return them for a sum agreed between themselves and the thieves."

"Yes, but they need to have a care,"

said Fulford, "or they can catch cold at that game. If they're caught with the goods in their possession, they're for the Nubbing Cheat, as felons call it. Remember Jonathan Wild?"

The notorious Jonathan Wild was a nursery tale familiar to most. He had pursued a successful life of theft and receiving stolen goods, while informing at the same time on his confederates to the authorities, thus earning the name of thief-taker. Eventually he was found out and hanged at Tyburn in 1725.

"Knew a man who recovered his watch and snuffbox by that means," put in Reade. "That was in London, though."

"Worth it, I should say," remarked Barnet. "Cut your losses. This Runner, now, he's investigating the murder at present, ain't he? Not that there's much likelihood he'll discover who did it — some chance intruder, it's said, whom the victim surprised. D'you suppose it could have been one of these thieves, after valuables at Denby House?"

"You've most likely hit the nail on the head there, Barnet," approved his host. "Not that I'm overjoyed to think that we've got those gentry in our vicinity! Not a word to my wife, I beg — she'll be in a horrendous state if she gets wind of it."

"But I should suppose the thieves would have removed from this neighbourhood with all speed once they discovered they'd killed someone," objected Fulford. "The game ain't worth the candle when murder's afoot."

"I'd agree with that, so you've nothing to worry over as far as your wife's concerned," soothed Reade. "Well, I'm off for some exercise. Anyone care to join me in a gallop?"

"I thought of going into York," said Fellowes. "I might buy myself some new cravats. My man complains that we didn't bring enough with us."

"Regret we've other plans for the afternoon, too," said Fulford, looking at Barnet.

Reade gave them a quizzical look. "After ladybirds again, are you? A certain house in Pavement, eh? Well, who's to blame you? Amuse yourselves, gentlemen."

Cholmondley hastened to cover up this

gaffe, and the five dispersed on their different errands.

Fellowes took his curricle into York, dispensing with the services of a groom for such a short distance. Once there, he stabled the vehicle at the Black Swan; going on foot to his ultimate destination, a street known as First Water Lane.

It was narrow and cobbled, with mediaeval and Tudor houses crowded along its steep gradient, which ran down to the river. The street was decidedly picturesque, although in a sleazy kind of way. Fellowes turned into it as one who knew his way; but he did look cautiously about him before entering a house next to one advertising ale and spirituous liquors.

His caution was not equal to the experience of Joseph Watts, who had arrived there in the company of the constable whom he had set on to follow Ross on the previous day. This worthy had duly reported that the man who had met Ross in the coffee house had left there soon afterwards and made his way to a dwelling in First Water Lane.

Watts had insisted on being shown

this street, which the constable had warned him was a rare haunt of crime. As luck would have it, he arrived there just as Fellowes was approaching the turning. Recognising the gentleman, Watts prudently concealed himself and the constable in a convenient doorway.

* * *

The Black Horse in Firsdale Village was a modest hostelry, certainly not in the posting inn class, but sufficiently respectable for the local gentry to patronise it on occasion, and for it to be a meeting place of most of their servants.

The landlord had been happy to oblige the Honourable Justin Rutherford, Quality from London, no less, and brother to Squire Marton's wife, by finding accommodation for Mr Joseph Watts, a respectable man with the kind of tidy domestic habits favoured by the landlord's wife.

"For put up with them folks as chucks their clobber all over t'place and worse when they'm drink taken, I'll *not*, no, not if tha asks on tha bended knees, Perkin, be it ever so! But yon lad — " this referred to Watts — "minds 'is manners, an' knows 'ow to treat a respectable female. What's more, he says he's never tasted owt so good as my apple pie, it puts him in mind of his ma's, poor lad."

Perkin, not as likely to be influenced by what he clearly saw as diplomatic remarks, acknowledged that Watts was a likeable fellow, and did not confide to his wife certain reservations about the man's occupation. Some of the servants from Denby House who were his customers had informed him of this, and Watts freely acknowledged it when they were sharing a friendly tankard of ale after breakfast on the morning following the interview at Denby House stables.

"Reckon y'know who I am?" Watts asked.

Perkin nodded. "Ay, reckon I do."

"Well, do me a favour, and don't spread the news around, friend. Some will know, o' course — the servants from Denby House, I reckon. Who else?"

The landlord considered.

"Groom from t'Squire's place, name o' Ross. Tak's a sup wi' t'Denby House lads, now an' then. In yestere'en, he were, along o' Jem, who's one on 'em. They was talkin' o' thee — I chanced to hear tha name in passing."

"Hm. That would have been after I'd been there to interview the head man, Webster, I reckon. Anyone else likely to know?"

Perkin shook his head. "Not yet, maister. But reckon t'word will spread afore long. Nowt's a secret here, sithee."

Watts nodded. "Yes, I'm taking account o' that. But meanwhile, they're more likely to open their mummers if they don't know, see? Reckon ye can help me, too, landlord, if ye've a mind to."

"Allus willin' to help the law," said Perkin, in pious tones.

Watts gave him a nod and a wink. "That's the dandy! Been here a long time, have you?"

"All o' twenty year. Bain't owt to do wi' me, maister Watts, but what zackly be ye lookin' for?"

"Murderer o' Sir Eustace Knowle," replied Watts, glibly.

The landlord considered him shrewdly for a moment.

"A burglar tryin' to break into t'Hall, that's what we all reckons in t'village. So tha thinks he'll still be hereabouts, dost tha? Why, maister?"

"I've got my reasons," replied Watts, darkly. "Don't do to open yer mummer too wide in my business. Tell me, now, what newcomers have there been in the neighbourhood lately — either servants in the big houses or other folk, cottagers, tradespeople and the like?"

The landlord whistled. "That's a tall order, maister. Still, I'll do my best. Tak' villagers first, as there's not many on 'em who've not been in Firsdale all their lives. There's Ned Appleton's niece at the post office, come to help his good lady out for a spell — "

"Don't bother about the females at present. I'm interested in males round about the age of forty."

"Is that a fact?" asked Perkin, with another shrewd look. "Well, no one comes to mind, then, barrin' a waiter and an ostler I took on extra for Races week, like, because o' t'extra gentry in t'neighbourhood. Recommended to me by t'landlord o' t'King's Arms in York — it's on t'King's Staith, sithee — he's a cove as I worked for, long ago. They'll be leavin' afore long, though, for I can't afford to pay out good brass for nowt, an' I reckon folk from Mr Cholmondley's place'll soon be gone."

Watts slid his notebook unobtrusively from his pocket.

"As those two will be about your premises, I suppose I can have a word with them just now? So that's the village people — what about new servants at the Quality houses locally? Take 'em one by one — Firsdale Hall, for instance? Any other than the two new grooms?"

Perkin shook his head. "Leckby and Ross — nay, there's none other there. Leckby's from t'Black Swan in Coney Street in York, sithee. Been there a good many years, but fancied a change for a bit. Ross — well — stable in Bradford, *he* says, sold up, so's he was forced to look elsewhere. Long way off, Bradford," he finished, ruminatively.

"Ay. Can ye tell me anything about the man? Ye say he comes in for a drink and a chat with the other local servants. Anything ye've noticed or heard about him?"

"We-ell, reckon he's a dab hand at sloping off," Perkin pronounced, after a pause. "Seems to get more time to 'isself than usual. Mostly he's out on errands — reckon he's quicker on t'uptake than t'other stable lads, so gets sent out more. But he knows how to tak' his time over t'business, he does an' all! And I reckon now an' then he does summat special for t'gennelmen stayin' with Mr Cholmondley. Saw him wi' one on 'em yesterday talkin' away serious like — brass changed hands, too."

"Which of the Warton Manor guests was this? Where, and when?" shot out Watts, pencil poised.

"Hold 'ard, maister! That gennelman called Fellowes, it was. And of all places in t'Black Swan, where I chanced to be on business. They wasn't together long, sithee, but seemed fair taken up wi' each other's chat. As for when, why reckon't would 'ave been close on one o'clock, judgin' by t'Little Admiral."

"Little Admiral?"

The landlord grinned. "Ay, Little Admiral atop t'clock o' St Martin le Grand in Coney Street, sithee."

"Ay, I know. It chances I was there at the same time, keeping an eye on our friend Ross. He did go into the Black Swan for a short spell, but I waited outside, so missed the meeting you saw. I'm too old a hand to be caught by a man entering a building to shake off pursuit — not that I think he'd spotted my surveillance, mind."

"Sounds as if tha'd got this Ross down for a villain?" queried Perkin.

"Only a suspect. In my trade, we suspect everyone, cully. But keep quiet on that, mind. So he was meeting this Mr Fellowes — interesting, very. And now, let's consider the other big houses. Any new staff there?"

"Denby House there's a new gardener — don't know his name, he's nobbut a lad. He's t'lad who found Sir Eustace Knowle's body, fair shook up ever since, he is. But if tha's only lookin' for men o' fortyish, he's no use. Warton Manor, now — " he frowned in recollection — "there's a couple o' lasses, kitchen maid and parlour maid — a footman — ”

Watts looked up. “Age?”

“Oh, ’bout t’reet age, I reckon, for thee. An’ then there’s a valet to Mr Fellowes — he’s not new, o’ course, only to t’house. He came wi’ his maister, as tha might expect.”

“Hm! Sounds promising. Tell me what ye can about the pair of ’em, if ye’d be so good, Perkin.”

The landlord drained his tankard and inspected the one in the Runner’s fist.

“Thirsty work, this, I reckon, maister. Happen tha’d like another?”

Watts thanked him, then waited while his host went towards the tap, returning with the tankards refilled.

“Not much I can tell,” he resumed, apologetically. “New footman was taken on three to four weeks agone. He’s been in t’tap wi’ other lads a few times — don’t seem much to say about him. Quiet like, not the sort as a body’d notice.”

“Where’s he from?”

“Did hear as ’ow t’maister hired him from one o’ them employment agencies in York, don’t know which. Reckon tha'd be able to find out? That's if it matters."

Watts nodded, making another note.

"This valet, now. Ye say he came to the Manor with Mr Fellowes — been in his service a while, then, I collect?"

Perkin spread his hands in a helpless gesture.

"No notion, maister. And he's only been in here once, sithee, with Mr Cholmondley's own valet, an' then they didn't stay above a half hour. Reckon he was wishful to see what it was like 'ere, and asked Mr Cholmondley's man to bring him along, because that one's never darkened my door afore. Reckon he tak's his sup o' ale in some crack York inn, along o' t'gentry."

"So you can't tell me anything about him? Never mind."

Watts had no great hopes of the valet as a suspect, since it appeared that the man must have been attached to the household of Mr Fellowes for some time. Nevertheless, he determined to see what he could glean from the housemaids at Warton Manor. As Justin had remarked, the Runner was adept at ingratiating himself with housemaids, thus gaining useful information.

"One other matter," resumed Watts, after a few moments' silence while both drank their ale meditatively. "Ye've been a great help, landlord, and I'm duly grateful. Now, I wonder if ye can find answers to a couple of points which are puzzling me? Mebbe not now — mebbe ye'll need to think," he added hastily, as he saw the other look troubled. "And mebbe ye can't help at all, which I'll fully comprehend, for ye're tied to your business, not out and about like most folk."

"Well, that's reet enough. What's tha want to know?"

"Cast your mind back to a week since, the night of the Lord Mayor's masquerade ball in York. Can ye recall who was here, in your hostelry, that evening — say, about nine o'clock?"

"Now tha's set me a puzzler, an' no mistake!" laughed Perkin. "Let me see, now — the reg'lars, I reckon, Bill Archer, Jem — "

"I'll make it simpler," cut in Watts, with no mind to hear a long list of names. "Was Ross one of 'em?"

This earned him another sharp glance.

"Ross, is it? Tha's a fancy for yon lad, sithee. Come to think on't — " he screwed up his eyes — "don't reckon he was. Nay, Ross wasn't there."

"Thankee. Another thing — have ye seen, yourself, or have ye heard tell of, anyone acting at all in an unusual way, or being somewhere ye wouldn't expect 'em to be, during the past week?"

Perkin shook his head slowly, looking puzzled.

"To give ye a notion of what I'm seeking," Watts expounded patiently. "Take the murder of Sir Eustace Knowle late on Tuesday night. Someone entered the grounds of Denby House, most like with felonious intent, and was surprised by the victim." This was the version for public information. "That person might well be one o' these newcomers to the neighbourhood ye've just now been telling me of. I say *might*, because equally it might be a complete stranger. But ye can see that it don't do for me to ignore any possible suspect, can't ye?"

Perkin nodded.

"That being so, if ye or any of your friends and neighbours saw anyone at all — but in particular any of these folk — acting suspiciously in the vicinity of Denby House on that night, I'd be obliged to hear of it. And not only on that night," the Runner added, choosing his words with some care. "If there's aught smokey going on hereabouts, no matter what, I'll trust ye to pass it on. Ye're in a fine position here as landlord to hear gossip, I'll be bound."

Perkin acknowledged that this was so, and promised to do his part in bringing the murderer to justice.

"But softly does it," warned the Runner, tapping the side of his nose. "One word in the wrong place, and the bird flies off, as we've learnt to our sorrow at Bow Street."

14

THE funeral of Sir Eustace Knowle passed off quietly on the Saturday, with no other members of the family present but Mrs de Ryde and her formidable sister-in-law, who had arrived post haste from Pickering on the previous day. The latter considered it her duty to be present at the interment, as her brother was still confined to his bed on doctor's orders; but her private view of the deceased fell lamentably short of that recommended by Christian charity.

On Sunday, the neighbours were relieved to see Mary de Ryde in church with Miss de Ryde, Anne and Miss Fawcett.

"One always feels better after the interment," whispered Mrs Cholmondley to her husband. "I don't know why it is, my dear, but it's always so."

Fanny Marton reflected compassionately that poor Anne looked monstrously forlorn in her blacks, and wondered if she would be permitted to attend the outing to Helmsley on Tuesday. Perhaps, she thought timidly, it would not be so *very* irreverent to address a prayer to the Almighty to that effect? She gazed at the new curate, and wished she might seek his guidance on that subject.

After the service, neighbours quietly offered their condolences to the afflicted lady who, protected by a thick black veil and the strong arm of Miss Cassandra de Ryde, managed to bear the ordeal without breaking down. They also asked after the health of her husband, and here Miss de Ryde took over the responses. Philip was making progress, slow but sure. Dr Clent said that a good constitution had guarded him from the worst effects of the concussion.

"As for bones, you know," she informed them in her sensible, no nonsense voice, "they take time to knit, of course. But since the damage is all on the left side, at least he has the use of his right arm. He was sitting up and taking nourishment yesterday, and if I know him, he'll be out of his bed tomorrow. We're not given to pampering ourselves in *my* family."

"D'you think he'd care for company, ma'am?" asked Sir George. "Not doing much visiting at present, but I'd like to look in if he feels equal to it."

Miss de Ryde gave it as her opinion that it would be the very thing to cheer up Philip, and called upon her sister-in-law to issue an invitation for that afternoon. To everyone's surprise, Mrs de Ryde rallied sufficiently not only to do so, but to include Julia and Fanny.

"You will forgive me, I know," she said, in a low tone, "if I do not also invite your nieces, but at present I don't feel equal to a large party. I know that Anne will be glad of your daughter Fanny's company, however, as they're accustomed to being so much together."

The rest of the Firsdale Hall party were in conversation with the Cholmondleys and their guests. By now, Justin had received a report from Watts on the activities of Fellowes in York on Friday, so was understandably curious about that gentleman.

"I collect from Cholmondley that you're interested in wandering around the town of York looking at its historic buildings, Mr Fellowes," he said. "There I think we may have an interest in common."

"Oh, yes, but indeed I can't lay claim to your scholarship, sir," protested the other. "I'm but a humble amateur."

"You're too modest, Fellowes," put in Barnet, with a grin at the others. "You gave us a vastly interesting, if lengthy, dissertation on Clifford's Tower the other day."

"You're pleased to roast me, Barnet, but I shan't regard it," replied the other, a shade petulantly.

"Everyone's fair game to Barnet," declared Fulford, digging Fellowes in the ribs. "He's a devil of a fellow for quizzing us all — haven't you noticed?"

Justin ignored this by-play. "Have you by any chance come across Mr Henry Cave's splendid book *Antiquities of York*?" he asked Fellowes. "He's included some delightful etchings of mediaeval and Tudor parts of the city. It was published a few years ago."

Fellowes replied regretfully that he had not, but would look out for a copy in the booksellers.

"One of the finest mediaeval streets, in my opinion," continued Justin, "is First Water Lane — have you been there, sir, at all?"

For a moment Fellowes looked taken aback. He quickly recovered, however, and admitted that he had.

"I took a short stroll along the street the other day. It certainly is, as you say, Mr Rutherford, vastly fine from a historic point of view, though somewhat delapidated."

"For my part," interrupted Reade, impatient of this scholarly discourse even on a Sunday after church, "my interest in York ends at the Knavesmire."

"Then I suppose you'll soon be returning home, Mr Reade, since the Races are over. What part of the country do you come from?" asked Rogers, carelessly.

"Oh, I've a place in the Midlands, but I'm seldom there," replied Reade, in the same tone. "Like Fellowes, I've a habit of travelling around to racecourses."

Further inquiry would have seemed impertinent, so Rogers was obliged to abandon what had been an attempt to assist Justin in his search into the origins of Cholmondley's guests. Justin had earlier tried to extract some information in a casual way from Cholmondley himself on this matter; but it had been abortive. The man neither knew nor cared who his visitors were or where their homes were situated. In one way or another, they had recommended themselves to him as good fellows, and that satisfied him. Justin had dropped a hint to Anthea that perhaps Mrs Cholmondley, who dearly loved a gossip, might be better informed. His niece promised to lose no opportunity of leading the lady on to reveal anything she knew.

"And I may say it's a prodigious sacrifice," she told him, "for a more boring creature I don't believe I ever encountered! Nevertheless, I'll do it for you."

"Fustian! You'll do it for yourself and the thrill of the chase, if I know you, my dear niece."

"Oh, well, perhaps. But, Justin, do you seriously think one of the Cholmondleys' guests is the murderer? I find it hard to believe that any of them could ever have been a transported convict."

"Especially not your favourite, Fulford?" he quizzed her, laughing at her indignation. "No, well, bear it in mind that our man has been an actor at one time, even if an unsuccessful one, so may have a few tricks of disguise and dissimulation up his sleeve. All I do know," he went on, more soberly, "is that any newcomer to the district whose origins are obscure and who's of the right age, must be suspect. He may be concealing himself among the humbler folk of the neighbourhood or among the gentry. Joe Watts is investigating the former possibilities, as you know. I don't intend to neglect the latter. These four men could fill the bill as far as age is concerned. Fulford appears a trifle younger than the others, but who can be sure? Moreover, we know nothing of them beyond what they choose to tell, which is precious little. Fellowes *says* he lives somewhere near Whitby, while Reade has named the Midlands — an immensely wide area."

But Anthea found no opportunity that morning for any private conversation with Mrs Cholmondley. Soon the groups dispersed to their carriages and she was left to rack her wits for some scheme to achieve this end. Perhaps it might be possible on the visit to Rievaulx Abbey.

* * *

"This is a damnable business, Philip," Sir George greeted his friend. "Y'might have been killed, old fellow."

The two were alone in de Ryde's bedchamber.

The patient was out of bed, as his sister had forecast, propped up with cushions on a sofa, with his left leg stretched out, splinted and bandaged, and his arm in a sling.

Philip de Ryde grimaced. "I feel as if I have been, George, tell you the truth. A devilish wreck I am now, hell and damnation to it!"

For a few minutes, Sir George commiserated with him, asking about the extent of the injuries and Dr Clent's prognosis.

"Oh, it'll take a devil of a time before I'm fully fit again, curse it! And God only knows why it should have happened — never been anything like it in my stable in the whole of my existence! I promise you, George, if ever I find out who's responsible — "

"The Runner looked into that. My brother-in-law, Justin sent him over here on Thursday evening. He was tolerably satisfied that none of your men had been negligent — "

"But, hell and the devil, I'm told the axle was tampered with! I saw Webster this morning — yes, I know, Clent was against my troubling my head with anything at present, but I had to know, dammit, George! Told me of the Bow Street man's visit, too. If my men weren't responsible — and I don't care to suppose that — then tell me who was?"

Sir George looked at him soberly.

"Whoever murdered Knowle."

"My God!" Philip de Ryde stared at him. "You think this was an attempt at — murder?"

Sir George nodded grimly. "Just as my supposed accident was. After all, we both received those threatening letters, did we not?"

"My God!"

De Ryde was silent for several moments.

"But how — when?"

"Who's to say? The Runner's guess is that someone broke into the carriage house overnight on Wednesday and did the mischief. Watts did have his eye on a groom from my stable who came over here with a message on Thursday afternoon, but it seems that fellow was ruled out. There was corroborative evidence."

"A message, eh? That reminds me — what did you want of me in such a hurry on Thursday evening? If I hadn't been rushing off in answer to your mysterious message, I shouldn't have been in this mess, I may tell you! And why did you particularly require me to bring the curricle? What was it all about, eh? Whatever it was, it's damn well gone by the board, now, I suppose."

Sir George started. "Message — what message?"

"The message you sent asking me to come immediately to your place, without loss of time, and to bring my curricle — come, man, you can't have forgotten!"

"You're sure," said his friend, carefully, "that this isn't a figment of your imagination brought on by the concussion you've suffered?"

"Dammit all, no! Figment of the imagination, indeed! If you don't believe me, ask m'wife's maid, Healey."

Sir George's eyes sharpened. "Healey? What's she to do with this?"

"She came into the bookroom to me with the message. George, d'you mean to say you never sent it?"

"That's precisely what I do mean to say. When did you receive this summons — at what hour?"

Philip de Ryde's face had not been in the pink of health when Sir George entered the room; now it was ghastly pale.

"I don't like this, old fellow, damned if I do! I can't be precise about the time, because I'd been reading, and y'know how it is — didn't notice. But I can tell you that I dashed off to the stables as soon as I was told, without troubling a groom to bring round the curricle, because I thought it would save time if I went myself. I'd not gone more than twenty yards or so down the drive before I was pitched out of the vehicle. That's the last I remember. But doubtless some of the staff — Healey, my head groom or one of the others — might have noticed what o'clock it was. Does it signify?"

The other man's expression was grim.

"It may signify a vast deal. If you don't mind, Philip, we'll have Healey in and question her about this."

"Of course, if you wish. Would you be good enough to ring for me? I hate being a damned cripple like this!"

Sir George hesitated for a moment, then appeared to make up his mind.

"Something I want to tell you first, old man. I know I can rely on you to keep this quiet — last thing we want is to make a stir in the neighbourhood. But there's more confirmation now of our belief that this evil business is the work of that villain Pringle who was transported for theft fourteen or more years since. You mentioned Healey. She's been threatened, too, and confessed to my niece on the day of your accident that she'd actually seen him once, briefly, on the night of the Lord Mayor's ball."

For a moment de Ryde was struck speechless.

"Y'know, George," he said, at length, "I couldn't help feeling that we might have conjured up all this out of our imagination — even after Eustace's murder, it seemed too fantastic for belief. But if Healey — "

He stopped, struck by a sudden thought.

"If she's seen the villain in person, then she must be able to identify him, for she knew him well enough in the past by all accounts."

Sir George explained, shaking his head. "And don't think she wasn't pressed hard on that point by my niece, who's alive on every suit, b'God! But the woman was quite firm that she wouldn't recognise him if she saw him again. Anthea said she was scared out of her wits at the mere thought of a further encounter — in a dreadful state."

"So that's what's been wrong with her lately. Mary's complained of the maid's fits of nerves, and said she might have to consider turning her off if she don't improve. Most likely will, now, in any event."

"Mayhap, but for the moment say nothing to your wife. As for Healey, d'you mind letting me deal with her? Know she's your servant, and all that, but I think we should have the interview on an official footing — that's if you've no objection, of course?"

"Only too relieved to be quit of it. Don't feel quite the thing yet — not equal to all this."

Accordingly Healey was summoned.

She came into the room with faltering steps, looking ready to swoon. After one glance at her, de Ryde ordered her to be seated. She collapsed thankfully on to an upright chair facing the two gentlemen.

"Sir George wishes to ask you a few questions, Healey," said her master. "Recollect that he is a Justice, and answer truthfully."

She inclined her head in acquiescence. Her hands were tightly gripped together in her lap.

"Nothing to be afraid of," began Sir George, reassuringly. "Your master tells me that you brought him a message on

Thursday afternoon, a message purporting to have come from me. At what time was this?"

"It — it was not long before the accident." Her voice was tremulous, and so weak they could scarcely hear.

"According to my niece, Miss Rutherford, the accident occurred at about a quarter to six. She was in conversation with you in the schoolroom at that time, and you'd been together for no more than ten minutes. Did you deliver the message to Mr de Ryde quite soon before being summoned to the schoolroom? Or was it earlier?"

"It — yes, quite soon. I'd — I'd just come from master when Miss Rutherford s-sent for me."

"I see. How did you receive this message?"

She gave a gulp, and lowered her eyes.

"One of your servants gave it me, y'r honour."

"A verbal message, I take it? Not written?"

She nodded.

"And the exact words — would you repeat them?"

"Mr de Ryde must come immediately to Firsdale Hall without delay, and be sure to bring his curricle."

She spoke without any hesitation this time, as if by rote.

"H'm." Sir George looked at de Ryde. "That's correct?"

The other man nodded, his eyes fixed on Healey.

"Who brought this message?"

She shook her head. "I don't know, y'r honour."

"You've been here at Denby House a good many years, Healey, and during that time there's been a deal of intercourse between the two households. You must be acquainted with many of my servants."

"It w-wasn't one I knew," she whispered.

"A new groom, perhaps? Did he give his name?"

"No, y'r honour."

"How long an interval did you allow to elapse between receiving the message and delivering it?"

"Straight away — I brought it straight away!"

There was a note of hysteria in her voice now.

"It seems unusual," mused Sir George, "that a message brought for the master of the house should have been delivered to the lady's maid rather than the butler or a footman. Can you explain why that was?"

She gave a moan and seemed about to swoon, but by a supreme effort pulled herself together.

"Because I wasn't indoors — I met him walking up the drive. I'd gone outdoors for a breath of air — oh, dear Lord, what can I do — what can I do?"

She broke down altogether, sobbing violently.

Sir George swore under his breath. He was a reasonably compassionate man, but this was a matter of murder and attempted murder. He must get at the truth; if he allowed the maid time to recover, it might be impossible to do so.

"D'you chance to have a vinaigrette in that apron pocket of yours? Use it, my good woman."

She obeyed him, groping blindly for the smelling bottle and holding it under her nose with a trembling hand. After several minutes, during which they surveyed her in silence, not unsympathetically, she seemed somewhat recovered.

"Now," said Sir George, firmly. "Let's make an end of this charade. We know that you have been threatened by the convict who was known here as Pringle fourteen years since. We know that messages have been passed between the two of you hidden in the temple in the grounds here. I believe that this story of yours concerning a servant from my staff bringing a message is nothing but a farrago of lies! The real truth is that you received one of these written instructions to convey that message to Mr de Ryde, pretending that it had come from me. Is that not true? Come, must I commit you to gaol before you confess?"

The scene which followed was painful. Healey, completely broken now, at length admitted that Sir George's assumption was correct. She had collected the instruction from the temple on the morning of Thursday, when Anne had chanced to see her; but she had delayed delivering it, fearing that it boded no good for her employer. Then, too scared for her own safety to disobey outright, she had been forced into doing the bidding of her tormentor.

"But I wouldn't have done it — no, I wouldn't, not if I'd known as it would cause master to have an accident! I'm feared — frit to death o' Pringle — I daresn't do other than what he says, for fear — oh, Gawd 'elp me! What'll ye do to me, y'r honour?"

"Nothing at present. On that other occasion, years ago, I judged you to be this villain's dupe rather than a criminal yourself. Now I see that you've been acting under duress, going in fear of your own life. One thing only I insist upon, in default of which you'll surely face criminal proceedings. You must give us all the assistance you can to uncover this murderer."

She promised eagerly, unable to believe that she had been fortunate enough to escape immediate punishment.

"I need to take this woman back with me to Firsdale Hall," Sir George said to his friend, "so that Justin and the Runner can interview her. Also, there's something they require her to do. It won't take more than an hour or so. Can it be managed without arousing curiosity, either on your wife's part or that of the other servants?"

This difficulty was resolved when Healey spoke up to say that Sunday afternoon was part of her off duty time, and therefore she could absent herself without question. She was dismissed, therefore, with instructions to don her bonnet and meet the Martons' carriage at the end of the drive in twenty minutes.

"The poor wench is between the devil and the deep blue sea," remarked Sir George, when she had gone. "I tell you, Philip, the more I see of crime, the more I wonder how great a part circumstance plays in it. But I'm no philosopher, and my duty is clear, at all events. We must catch this murderer by any means at our disposal."

15

WHEN the Martons returned home, they found Giles Crispin sitting with Anthea and Louisa. It seemed that he had called in the hope of taking Louisa out for a drive; but in spite of her cousin's strong encouragement, she had not ventured to accept without her aunt's permission.

This Julia gave, though somewhat reluctantly; and after a few moments of polite interchanges, the pair departed.

"Really, I don't at all know what I ought to do about Louisa," complained Julia in a worried tone. "My sister Harvey is quite set on a match between her and the Thirkells' eldest son, whom they've known this age. Indeed, Celia tells me that they are as good as affianced, only that for some reason the young man hasn't yet come up to scratch."

Anthea laughed. "I wondered why you seemed so unwilling to consent to the outing, as the gentleman appears to be quite unexceptionable and is well known to you. But matches made by mamas don't always suit the notions of their offspring, Aunt! If the Thirkell gentleman seems reluctant — and anyone may see that Louisa isn't breaking her heart over that! — then why not leave be? I dare wager that it will all turn out for the best in the long run."

"That's all very well, Anthea, but I feel in some sort responsible. A fine thing it will be if Celia suspects me of interference, promoting the interests of Mr Crispin against those of her chosen *parti*! She may think that I should prevent Louisa from seeing too much of him."

"Nonsense, m'dear," put in Sir George. "The Crispins are our neighbours, so you can't prevent the chit from meeting the boy whenever they call on us. As for their driving out together on a fine summer afternoon — well, young men like to be seen out with a pretty girl, and where's the harm?"

"Where, indeed?" put in Rogers, an unexpected ally. "I was about to suggest the very same thing to Miss Anthea, but with what success I can't say."

Julia smiled, having no possible objection to *this* scheme.

"Were you indeed?" said Anthea, lifting her eyebrows at him.

"Would you care for a spin?" he repeated, in a much humbler tone.

"Thank you," she replied, graciously, "that would be most pleasant." She rose from her chair. "I'll be ready in just a few minutes."

"A likely tale!" scoffed Justin, as Rogers rose to open the door for her.

She wrinkled her nose at her offending relative, but rewarded his friend with a bright smile that set his pulses racing.

"By the way," Justin said to Rogers when she had gone, "see that you don't take that groom Ross with you. Watts and I have other plans for the remainder of his afternoon."

In spite of Justin's scepticism, Anthea returned in a very short time, as promised, having donned what Rogers considered a bewitching bonnet of yellow corded silk trimmed with white flowers. Its wide brim made a frame for her piquant face and mop of black curls, while the yellow ribbons tied under her left ear added to the saucy look.

Justin pursed up his lips in silent, mocking appreciation, and she only just managed to repress a schoolgirl impulse to put out her tongue at him.

"Very pretty, m'dear," approved Sir George.

Rogers shepherded her out to the waiting curricle, handing her up solicitously before mounting into the vehicle himself and taking up the reins. The groom who had been holding the horses, a matched pair of chestnuts, released them and swung himself up into the dickey behind.

"I can't tell you how glad I am to be out of doors," said Anthea, as they went down the drive and turned into the narrow lane which led to the highway. "Louisa and I were about to go for a stroll when Mr Crispin called, but after that we had to sit about in the parlour while I tried to persuade Louisa that there could be no possible objection to her going for a drive with him. She is a dear, but vastly over timid, to my way of thinking."

"An accusation that couldn't be levelled

at you, I think?" he ventured, smiling down at her.

"Well, I should hope not. One misses a vast deal of fun if one is — but, of course, one would not wish to exceed the bounds of propriety," she added, demurely.

"Dear me, no. That would never do."

She glanced at him suspiciously, but he returned her look with one of bland innocence.

"I sometimes think," she said severely, "that you're trying to roast me, Mr Rogers! Do you take anything I say seriously, I wonder! Oh, how will we manage now?"

This exclamation was caused by the appearance of a horseman coming towards them. As the lane was barely wide enough to accommodate the curricle and pair, it was not an unreasonable question, and was echoed in the groom's mind.

"Quite adequately, I believe," Rogers replied, calmly.

She sat perfectly still, watching as he guided the horses expertly into the nearside of the lane so that his equipage missed the hedge by only a few inches.

This allowed the horseman comfortable room to pass, which he did with a bow of thanks, doffing his hat.

"Oh, splendid!" she said, impulsively. "I wish you might teach me to drive like that!"

"With the greatest pleasure in the world," he answered, as he turned into the high road. "Would you care for a lesson now?"

"*Would* you trust me with your horses? I don't think Justin would, though I *am* quite a good whip, he says. It's illogical of him, isn't it, if he truly does think so? But of course men are monstrous touchy about their horses, are they not?"

He nodded. "Yes to all three questions," he said, laughing. "But do you wish to try your hand at the chestnuts? They may be a trifle fresh."

"Oh, I take no heed of that! Yes, perhaps I will tool them along a little — they're such splendid animals, it would be quite a feather in my cap to tell Justin I had driven them!"

He looked at her bonnet, smiling. "A feather would quite spoil the effect. But by all means let us change over."

He reined in, signalling to the groom to come to the horses' heads. In a few moments, Anthea was seated in his place, the reins in her hands, while he took the passenger side.

He set his mouth a little as she gave the horses the office to start, for he had never previously seen her driving, although he knew she was an excellent horsewoman. There was a vast difference, however, between riding a horse and managing a pair harnessed to a vehicle. He told himself that he must appear relaxed, while being ready for any emergency.

In ten minutes, he had relaxed completely. Anthea was handling the chestnuts confidently, and they appeared to recognise the fact.

"I suppose I dare not utter a word of praise," he remarked, after they had travelled several miles, "or you'll think I'm patronising you."

She shook her head, guiding the equipage neatly past a farm waggon.

"I'm not so mean spirited, I hope. Yes, pray do tell me how pleased you are with my driving! You know how I dote on flattery!"

"I know how you pretend to do so," he countered. "If you think to gammon me, I must warn you that you're mistaken."

At that moment, a curricle came towards them, steering an uncertain course which seemed sure to bring the two vehicles into collision.

At once, Rogers placed firm hands over Anthea's on the reins, forcing his horses well over to the left. They tossed their heads rebelliously, but responded to his guidance until they had safely passed the other curricle.

He pulled in to the side of the road, shouted to the groom to go to the horses' heads to quieten them, and leapt angrily to the ground. The driver of the other curricle had also pulled up, and was waiting for him.

"What the devil d'you mean by careering all over the road in that fashion?" Rogers demanded. "You might have caused an accident! Are you foxed, man, or what?"

He saw then that the offending driver was none other than Sir John Fulford, looking very pale and more than a little apologetic. The groom sitting beside him was in no better state.

"Beg pardon, I'm sure, sir," Fulford began. Then recognising Rogers — "B'God, it's you, Mr Rogers — and Miss Rutherford! 'Pon my soul, I'm mortified — can't tell you how sorry I am! Fact is, I don't feel too well — something I ate at nuncheon, I daresay — "

He broke off, evidently in some physical distress.

Rogers, considerably mollified by the sight, spoke more quietly.

"I see that you're unwell. I suggest you allow the groom to drive you back to the Manor. I trust you'll soon be recovered. Good day to you."

He returned to his own vehicle to find that Anthea had stepped down and had been regarding with interest the exchange between himself and Fulford.

"Well!" she exclaimed, as they resumed their seats, this time with Rogers driving. "What was that all about? Do you suppose he was — well — bosky?"

Justin would have quibbled at the word, but Rogers took no such liberties. He was bent on staying in the lady's good books.

"Let's give him the benefit of the doubt," he answered, diplomatically. "He said it was something he'd eaten."

Anthea looked back. "He's done as you suggested, and let his groom drive," she reported, "and they're turning back."

"He may go to the devil for all I care! Let's forget about him and continue to enjoy our outing. Would you perhaps care to take a stroll presently? We'll come to a pleasant wooded stretch about a mile from here."

Anthea agreed enthusiastically to this suggestion. Soon they pulled up at a gate leading into the wood, and left the equipage to the care of the groom until their return.

There was a path leading through the wood wide enough to take two abreast. For a time they walked in silence amid the sunlight dappled trees, savouring the cool remoteness of their refuge from the heat of August. A rabbit started from the undergrowth, scuttering across their path with a flash of short white tail.

It made Anthea start and clutch at her companion's arm for a moment. He closed his hand over hers, looking into her eyes.

"Miss Anthea!" he murmured. "Oh, Anthea, my dear!"

They stood still. She found herself breathing deeply, as if she had been running. Under his intense gaze, her whole being seemed to melt. What message her hazel eyes gave him, she could not tell, but he must have read some acquiescence there. He gathered her into his arms, and their lips met.

For several moments they remained in a close embrace; then she gently detached herself, standing back, but still clasping his hands. Her bonnet had fallen to the back of her head, held only by its ribbons.

"Anthea, my dearest!"

He made as if to take her in his arms again, but she shook her head, smiling.

"I love you," he said, his grey eyes deep and serious. "Do you — can you possibly — return my feelings, dearest girl?"

The mischief had vanished from her own eyes.

"I — I believe I can," she said, in a low tone.

His voice caught on a note of exultation; this time, he would not be denied, sweeping her once more into a strong embrace. She reciprocated eagerly, with no pretence of maidenly shrinking.

Presently, she pushed him gently away.

"We must go — the groom will be awaiting us, and Aunt Julia will not like it if we're too long absent," she reminded him.

"Oh, confound the rest of the world! But I suppose you're in the right of it," he conceded, reluctantly. "Since we must, let us turn back, then."

He placed an arm about her waist, and together they retraced their steps.

"I'll speak to your father as soon as your parents return from their visit to the Lakes," he said, jubilantly. "How soon will you marry me, dearest?"

"I — I don't know," she said, hesitantly. "I'm not sure that I want to enter the married state immediately."

He stopped in his tracks, consternation in his face.

"Not be married! But then — you do

love me, Anthea, don't you? There's no mistake on my part?"

"Yes, I do," she said, firmly. "But no — you mustn't embrace me again, for we need to talk seriously, to understand each other."

He drew back, checking the instinctive movement to take her again in his arms, and looking down at her with a hurt expression.

"Understand each other? But what is there to understand beyond our love and its natural outcome in marriage?"

She sighed. "Yes, it *is* difficult to explain. But, you see, Sidney — " it was the first time she had used his name, and he thrilled to it — "I fear I'm rather a contrary female! There are so many things I would like to do before I settle down to being a staid married lady — even with you," she added, looking shyly up at him. "I want to travel overseas — "

"But I'll take you! Tell me where — we can go there for our bridal visit!"

She shook her head. "Yes, that would be delightful, too, but it isn't quite what I mean. I want to discover places — and things — for myself, and by myself. I want — oh, I don't know quite what I do want, except that I wish to be free for just a little longer! Can you understand that? Please say you do! Please, dear Sidney!"

"What I do understand," he answered, in a deeply mortified tone, "is that you don't feel for me as I for you, and you are giving me my *congé*. Very well, I can't do other than accept. Allow me to apologise for having pestered you on this subject. I promise not to return to it again."

"Oh!" she cried, breaking away from him and running ahead out of the wood. "Men are beyond anything *stupid*!"

* * *

"No harm can possibly come to ye, Mrs Healey, none whatsoever," Watts assured the trembling maid. "Two of us here to take care of ye. Now just sit ye down on yon stool, and I'll leave the door open a crack, not enough for him to see ye, but so's ye can hear his voice. All ye have to do, wench, is *listen* — just listen, and if ye recognises that voice, make a sign to Mr Rutherford here, beside ye. A nod will do — no need to speak. D'ye understand?"

She nodded, sitting down as directed, but still looking frightened, in spite of the reassuring presence of Justin at her side.

She had been brought surreptitiously to a small shed in the kitchen garden lit only by a single pane of glass in its roof. At this time on a Sunday the garden was deserted, so they were quite free from observation.

In spite of the fact that Justin had a spare, athletic frame, he seemed to fill all the available space in the shed. A cobweb caught in his unruly hair. He brushed it aside impatiently.

"Devilish place this, Joe," he complained. "My sister'll have a fit if she catches me before I've had a chance to wash and brush up, so don't be too long about this, there's a good chap."

At that moment a footstep sounded approaching along the gravel path, so he froze into silence. Watts positioned himself in an easy stance in front of the door, which was almost closed.

It was Ross who came up to the waiting Runner.

He touched his cap respectfully.

"You wanted me, sir?"

Watts nodded.

"Ay. Thought we'd have a chat where we could be on our own. Ye know about the accident to Mr de Ryde, of course?"

Ross nodded. "Very sorry to hear it, sir."

"Ay. Understand ye took a message to Denby House for the master there not long before it happened — message from Sir George. That correct?"

"Yessir. About four o'clock it would be. Don't know what time the accident 'appened, though."

"Who did you give the message to?"

"The butler, sir."

Watts nodded. So far, all this confirmed what he had previously discovered from Kirby and Sir George himself. The note had been a friendly message from Sir George to say that he would call in at Denby House on the following day if de Ryde would like to receive him. He had written it before going off to the

Knavesmire with his family, instructing that one of the grooms might deliver it at any time convenient to Carr, the head groom.

Watts was interested to observe that Ross, although reputedly coming from Bradford, had no trace of the Yorkshire accent. Indeed, his speech was more that of an upper servant than a groom, with the occasional lapse of a dropped aitch. He seemed quite composed.

"Did ye rcturn straight arterwards to y'r duties?"

Ross hesitated. "Well, p'raps not quite — I stayed to talk to some of the stable lads I know, for a bit."

"I see. Earlier that day, ye were sent to York on an errand."

"Yessir — to the saddler's."

Watts was silent for a few moments, steadily regarding the groom. Ross began to fidget under the scrutiny, looking less sure of himself.

"The saddler's — yes," Watts continued. "And then ye looked in at the Black Swan in Coney Street."

Ross repressed a start, but said nothing, barely giving a nod to this. Watts, who had no intention of showing all his hand, deliberately abandoned that topic.

"And then ye went on to a coffee house in the alley beside that red devil statue in Stonegate. Managed a fair old tour of the town, didn't ye? Who was the cove ye met there?"

He shot out the final sentence abruptly. This time Ross could not manage to conceal his dismayed surprise.

"A — a friend," he replied, haltingly. "No one in particular."

"Not been here long, have ye? Matter o' six weeks or so? Not much time to make friends in the town."

"I — we — that's to say," Ross said, desperately, "we knew each other afore. He's from Bradford."

"Oh, yes? And his moniker? I suppose he's got one," Watts added, with heavy sarcasm.

The groom made a strong effort to pull himself together.

"His name's Teasdale, sir. But what's all this about — are you accusing me of anything? It 'bain't a crime to meet a friend when a cove's out on an errand, surely? Mayhap I did waste a bit of the master's time, but they don't set Runners on to you for that these days, do they?"

Once again, Watts had no intention at this stage of revealing the full extent of his knowledge about the groom's encounters with others.

"Ye watch y'r mummer," he warned. "No, they don't waste our time with small fry like y'rself unless ye start tryin' to swim in the big pool. Have a care, lest ye get gobbled up, my fine cully. That's all — sling yer hook."

Ross departed smartly on this command, without once looking back.

When he had quite disappeared, Justin pushed open the shed door and emerged, brushing his coat.

"No good," he said, briefly.

"Ye didn't recognise his voice?" Watts asked Healey, disappointed.

She stood up, also coming out into the open.

"No, it was nothing like," she said, in a firmer voice than they had heard from her lately. "He's not the man. I can swear it."

* * *

"And how d'ye like it there, m'dear?" asked Watts, all benevolent interest.

The Cholmondley's new parlourmaid blushed and lowered her eyes.

"Oh, Mr Watts! Tha shouldn't talk like that, not when tha's only known me a few days!" she protested, though not very strongly.

"Long enough to find out as ye *are* a dear. And if so, why shouldn't I say so?" he demanded.

"Oh, thee lads from Lunnon be as bold as brass! What's a lass to do with thee?"

He gave her a sly glance. "Shall I tell ye, m'dear?"

She replied that he was a terror and no mistake; for a few moments the badinage followed its age-old pattern. Presently, Watts persuaded her to reply seriously to his original question.

"Oh, its a'reet. Madam an' maister's very easy goin'. T'housekeeper's a bit o' a besom, but I can get round t'butler, I reckon. T'rest o' t'staff is a'reet."

"What about the house guests? D'ye

get any trouble from them?"

She pursed her lips. "Well, that Sir John Fulford pinches my — tak's liberties, sithee. It don't do to meet him in a dark corner. Don't see much on t'others."

"Married men, would ye say?"

"An' 'ow should I know, think on?" she asked him pertly. "I don't even know if tha's wed thysen!"

"Heart whole an' fancy free — at least, until I met you."

"Oh, I never! Mr Watts, behave thysen!"

It took several minutes after this to steer the conversation back to the Cholmondleys' guests, but he managed it skilfully at last.

"Well, I don't reckon as any on' em's wed," she pronounced. "No wife'd put up wi' 'em bein' away all t'time. What's more, two on 'em, any road, goes off to — " she blushed again — "to them 'ouses wi' a bad name, sithee. In a street called Pavement, so I 'eard tell."

"Which two would that be, my charmer?"

She gave him a coy glance before naming Fulford and Barnet.

"Reade and Fellowes don't join 'em, then?"

She shook her head. "Though they both go out o' night times, when maister's not entertaining."

"D'ye know when, my pretty? Last Tuesday, for instance?"

She reprimanded him again before she condescended to pause and consider the question.

"They'd bin to Knavesmire in t'day," she said, slowly. "Arter dinner, maister took 'em all into York to some club or other. They goes there often. Madam don't 'ave much of a life, I reckon, 'appen that's why she likes entertaining."

"Ye wouldn't know what time they returned home that evening?"

She glanced at him, a faint suspicion dawning; fortunately, she was not very bright.

"Arter I was abed, any road. Only male staff stays up late, an' p'raps madam's personal maid at times."

He judged that it was wiser to ask no more questions at present about the house guests. At any rate, he felt he had laid some foundation for the future.

16

ON the following morning, Rogers made his excuses to his host and hostess. A letter he had just received — he waved it casually in one hand — had called for his presence at home in Sussex immediately.

"Oh, dear," remarked Julia, sympathetically. "Not, I trust, bad news about the health of either of your parents?"

"No, no, ma'am, nothing of that nature," he reassured her. "Simply a business matter which must be attended to promptly, I fear, and can't be dealt with in my absence. I regret infinitely being obliged to leave you, and at such short notice. It has been a prodigiously pleasant stay — would that I could prolong it. I can't thank you sufficiently for your generous hospitality."

"Which was all very well," pronounced Julia to the others, when their guest had taken leave of them all and departed, "but what does it signify, I wonder? Are you perhaps able to throw any light on the matter, Anthea?"

"I, Aunt?" replied her niece, in well simulated surprise. "Why should you suppose I know anything of Mr Rogers's concerns? You should rather address your questions to Justin, I imagine."

She went out of the room with an air of having pressing affairs to attend to elsewhere.

Julia sighed. "I feel sure those two have quarrelled, Justin, though why in the world they should, quite passes my comprehension! Do you know anything — has Rogers confided in you?"

Justin gave a wry smile. "And if he had, m'dear sister, you couldn't suppose I'd do anything so shabby as to betray his confidence? Very well — " he threw up his hands in a defensive gesture as she advanced threateningly — "yes, I do know something, and no, I don't mean to tell you about it, I think you will know as well as I do that no good ever comes of meddling in affairs of that nature — leave it all to the healing influence of time, eh, George?"

"Oh, ay, decidedly," agreed his brother-in-law, without the slightest hesitation.

"Well, it is all vastly tiresome," declared Julia, accepting that she would get no more from her brother. "There's the play this evening, for one thing. It's to be Miss Campbell in *The School For Scandal*, and he did say that he was looking forward to that. However, I suppose people will have their whims."

Anthea herself made no reference to Sidney Rogers. She passed the rest of the day by riding with Louisa in the morning, and sitting quietly in the parlour with her aunt during the afternoon, a book in her hand to preclude conversation. Louisa alone noticed that her cousin seldom turned a page; but she was a discreet girl, and made no mention of this.

That same morning Perkin, landlord of the Black Horse in Firsdale village, had been imparting some interesting information to Joseph Watts.

"Tha said to let 'ee know when I heard owt in tha line o' business, maister Watts, so I reckon there's a couple o' things I can tell 'ee. They do talk, an' no mistake, when they've 'ad a drop. One o' t'lads from Mr de Ryde's stable let slip that 'e 'eard a noise arter 'e was abed over t'vehicle shed t'night afore his maister's accident. Only bein' as 'e was nobbut 'arf awake and not minded to see what was afoot, 'e told 'imself it were nowt but rats. But since tha's been there questionin' 'em, he's 'ad second thoughts — not what I'd call a quick thinkin' lad at best, sithee."

"Oh, he has, has he?" repeated Watts grimly. "Well, reckon I'll have a word with that cully. What d'ye say his moniker is?"

"Bill Mott," supplied Perkin. "Tha'll likely 'ave spoken to 'im when tha was there afore. But that's not all, Mr Watts — tha said to tell 'ee o' anyone bein' seen actin' suspicious like, or where they'd no business to be. Well, I've 'eerd tell o' a coupla queer things — might be nowt in 'em, think on, but reckon tha should know about 'em."

"Quite right, and I'm grateful for your help, landlord. Now, what exactly have ye heard?"

"Firstly, one o' t'footmen at Mr de

Ryde's says as 'ow the valet thought he saw someone peerin' in at t'French window at Denby House on t'night o' t'murder. He couldn't be sure because he was at t'bedroom window above, and 'is eyes 'bain't too good, sithee. But if Sir Eustace was killed by a burglar, 'appen that was t'bloke, 'anging about waitin' to break in."

Watts nodded. "Not much help to us now, though."

He reserved the opinion that it might equally have been the man who was planning the murder.

"I reckon not, but there's more to come," said Perkin, in a slightly deflated tone. "Goin' back to t'afternoon o' Mr de Ryde's accident, one o' t'gardeners at Firsdale Hall reckons he saw a gennelman slippin' in to t'grounds o' Denby House by t'side gate leadin' from t'lane between t'two."

"What gennelman?" snapped Watts.

Perkin shook his head. "That he can't say, Mr Watts, try ever so, as I did mysen. He 'bain't more'n sixpence in t'shilling, think on."

"I'll see him nonetheless — his name?"

The landlord supplied it, and Watts made a note.

"Anything more?"

"Well, ay, reckon so," said Perkin, slowly. "Tha did ask about t'night o' Lord Mayor's ball, wantin' to know if anyone'd been seen around these parts where they 'adn't ought to be. I don't reetly know where this 'elps 'ee, but reckon it's worth tellin'. Someone else saw a gennelman makin' use o' that there gate to Denby House latish on that night — leastways, 'e might not 'ave been a gennelman, but 'e was wearin' a cloak, which was all this bloke could make out, seein' as it was dark."

"Now that *is* useful," said Watts, approvingly. "I'll need to know this man's moniker, too."

"Well, mebbe that's a mite difficult," Perkin demurred. "This bloke was up to no good himself that night, sithee — in fact, he's a poacher. Not that owt's ever been proved, tha knows — but he'll not thank me for puttin' t'law on him, an' I've to think on my trade, sithee."

"Yes, well, ye deserve to have something overlooked, seeing that ye've been helping in the King's business. Tell ye what, persuade this cully to come here and have a word with me, and no questions asked about his own doings that night. Eh?"

Perkin said doubtfully that he would do his best, and would let Watts know if and when it was possible to make an appointment.

"But I doubt tha'll get any more from 'im than what I've told 'ee — come to that, I don't reckon any on 'em can tell more. I asked 'em a mort o' questions mysen, think on."

Watts soothed the landlord's injured pride by saying that he had done splendidly, and that doubtless no more could be learned by further questions.

"But it's my business to put 'em personally, ye see, no matter how reliable my informant. In the meantime, I know I can rely on ye to keep your eyes skinned, and your mummer shut, eh?"

On this friendly note they parted.

Watts spent the rest of the morning following up the landlord's information, but at the end of it all learned nothing further. As he had expected this kind of result, he was not unduly discouraged.

He contrived a brief meeting with Justin in the afternoon to pass on the information.

"Don't take us much further, I fear, guv'nor, though it confirms some of our theories," he said apologetically. "That groom Mott, for instance, who says he heard someone in the stable the night afore Mr de Ryde's accident — well, we reckoned that's the way the curricle was tampered with. One thing, though, strikes me, and that's this mention of *gentlemen* being seen on two suspicious occasions, using the side gate access to Denby House. The gardener at the Hall — more'n a bit slow in the uptake, I'll admit, guv'nor — but swore on the good book that it *was* a gennelman, and no ordinary labouring cove as he saw. Tried to shake him, but he stood firm on that, though he couldn't identify him."

"But the other witness, the poacher, you've not interviewed yet? He could have been mistaken — after dark, y'know."

"True, sir, though I reckon only the gentry wears cloaks. I'm anxious to have a word with that cully, see if I can learn more. But if they're both in the right of it, and they did see a gennelman — well, guv'nor, I don't need to say more."

"Indeed not. Healey was threatened in the temple by a man wearing a cloak and mask on the night of the Lord Mayor's ball. That man *could* have been going to the ball as a guest, if this poacher is correct in identifying him as one of the gentry. *Ergo* — but I don't need to underline the conclusion, Joe, not to you. The time seems to fit what Healey told us, though perhaps when you interview the man he can verify this."

Watts nodded. "The only newcomers to the district who're gentry are Mr Cholmondley's guests, sir — yes, that's for certain sure. And we do have our eye on one of those guests already."

"Agreed, but yet I don't know . . . we must find out more about them, by hook or crook. I hope to achieve something in this way tomorrow on the excursion to Rievaulx, but in the meantime I wonder if you can do a little snooping, Joe? There's that pretty housemaid of yours at Warton Manor — could she smuggle you into their quarters, do you suppose, while they're all absent from the house? There must be some clues to identity lying about in their bedchambers — letters, other papers, even possessions which give a hint?"

Joseph Watts pulled a face. "Most irregular, guv'nor, as ye very well know."

"But often necessary for the ends of justice," countered Justin. "Very well, I'll admit I don't in general favour the Jesuitical approach! Only this is murder, and there might be more yet."

Watts winked. "Bless ye, guv'nor, I was only pullin' your leg, but I reckon ye know that."

* * *

In the evening all the Firsdale Hall party with the exception of Sir George, whose injury was a deterrent to social outings, and Harry, who acknowledged he was bored by dramatic performances, set out for the Theatre Royal.

Justin made no complaint about being required to squire three females without a companion of his own sex, but he found himself missing Rogers. He had a shrewd notion that he was not the only one.

The party alighted from their carriage at the entrance in Lop Lane, and were ushered into the box which Sir George reserved permanently for his use, although that was not very frequent. Anthea glanced around the theatre as the others were arranging themselves on the crimson covered chairs, and approved its classic style.

"Do you notice who our neighbours are?" Justin whispered, as he took a seat beside her.

Anthea glanced quickly at the next box, then away again.

"I might have known," she replied, in the same tone, "from the hubbub! Mrs C never can do anything without making a piece of work about it, can she?"

The criticism was not unfounded. Directions were being issued by the minute to the hapless visitors whom the Cholmondleys had brought with them.

"Pray sit here, Mr Barnet — no, I do not think you will see so well there — let my husband take that chair! My dear, you will not mind being a little to one side, I know — " this to her husband — "and you may have that chair, Mr

Fulford — oh, no, but then you will be in Mr Reade's way — "

"No matter to me, ma'am," replied that gentleman, gallantly. "Truth to tell, I'm not vastly addicted to play going, and shall most likely drop off in the middle."

She protested at this and began on another bout of directions. As it was all plainly audible to the boxes on either side of them and caused some amusement, it was treated almost as an extra performance.

Presently they were all seated to her satisfaction and she had leisure to look about her. Her eye at once alighted on the occupants of the neighbouring box, and she uttered a cry of delight.

"Lady Marton! Now if this isn't beyond anything extraordinary, as we so rarely attend the play! Only with this being quite the most popular of Mr Sheridan's pieces — so sad about his death, you know, but we all must go some time, I suppose — and then our visitors found themselves with nothing in particular to do, so we thought it a good opportunity for them to see our theatre — "

She was leaning over the edge of the box, speaking in a voice that carried to everyone nearby. Fortunately, a good many others in the auditorium were also cackling away, as Justin phrased it, so no one took much notice.

Julia soon managed to staunch the flow of her conversation by saying that they would all meet in the lobby during the intervals, and everyone was able to settle down for the performance.

The floodgates were opened again, however, when the first interval arrived. Mrs Cholmondley enthused indiscriminately about the performers, Julia and Anthea having to bear the brunt of her raptures, as Cholmondley was chatting to Louisa.

Sir John Fulford made his usual attempt to place himself close to Anthea; but this time her reception of him was so extremely cool as to dampen even his ardour. Evidently she preferred the company of his hostess.

"The lady's not in a receptive mood," said Barnet in low tones. "You'll do no good there at present."

"Did myself no good yesterday," admitted Fulford, glumly. "Met her out for a drive with that chap Rogers — must admit I was a bit on the go and driving cow handedly."

"Half seas over, old fellow, by my recollection," retorted Barnet, grinning.

Fulford grimaced, resigning himself to conversing with Justin, who had that moment joined the group.

"How are you enjoying the play?" Justin inquired of the group. "Doubtless you'll have seen it before, I dare say."

All except Reade assented, though Barnet and Fulford both admitted that it was some years since.

"I suppose you'll have seen it in London," Justin continued. "At which theatre — the Lane or the Garden?"

"Yes, certainly in London," agreed Fulford, "though damme if I can recall where."

"Would it have been since they were both rebuilt after the fires? It was a cruel stroke of fate, was it not, that both should have been burnt down within a short time of each other — Covent Garden in the autumn of '08 and Drury Lane in the following spring. If you do chance to have been to a performance in the new buildings, what did you feel about the enlargement of the auditorium? It seems to me that nowadays a sense of closeness and intimacy between actors and audience is missing, very different from the old days when I was up at Oxford and attended performances occasionally."

"I haven't been to either since the reconstruction," said Barnet, "but I'd agree it's essential to be able to see the actors' facial expressions, as so much is conveyed in that way. If this is lost in the present buildings, I'd agree it's a devilish shame! What say you, Fellowes? You've been there, I expect."

"Well, I'm seldom in London, as I've told you, but I do chance to have attended performances at both the new theatres. Yes, you may be in the right of it, though I hasten to add that I'm no true judge."

"I can't lay claim to being an ardent follower of the drama any more than these two," put in Fulford with a shrug. "The play's the thing, as that fellow Shakespeare said, I think — but as to watching actors' expressions, well, I'm tolerably satisfied if they only leap about the stage enough."

"Like Edmund Kean?" suggested Justin, smiling.

Fulford and Barnet appeared nonplussed, he noticed, while Reade merely continued to look as bored as he had done throughout the conversation. It seemed that the actor's name meant nothing to them. Fellowes, however, was better informed.

"That chap who made his first appearance a couple of years back, and was a prodigious hit? Never seen him myself, but, as I say, I'm seldom up in London these days."

"There are one or two taking bits of muslin here," whispered Fulford to Barnet. "Over there, look, filly in the aquamarine gown and her companion — approachable, would you say?"

"Don't think they're bits of muslin," declared Barnet, after a quick glance. "Moreover, there's a damned unpleasant looking fellow escorting them."

"Just our luck," Fulford shrugged.

The interval bell sounded, and there was a general scramble to resume seats.

Noticing that Fellowes was hanging well back from his party, Justin moved over to Anthea; after a quick whispered word in her ear, he detached himself from the others and entered the cloakroom.

As he had hoped, no one was within but a bored attendant almost asleep in his chair. Justin left the door open a crack through which he could see into the lobby, then when the audience had quite dispersed, he cautiously emerged.

There was no sign of Fellowes.

He ran lightly down the staircase into the foyer. No one was about here, either, since the performance had now resumed. He moved quickly to the entrance door and passed through into the street. It was dusk outside. He moved cautiously round the corner into narrow Lop Lane, away from the lights of the theatre.

A quick glance showed him two men standing in conversation against the wall. At once he drew back into the shadow of an adjacent doorway, straining his eyes to identify them.

The plump outline of Fellowes presented little difficulty, but it was several moments before he could make out who his companion might be.

When he did, it came as no surprise to realise that it was Ross.

The groom had accompanied the party from Firsdale Hall on the box of their coach. Fellowes and Ross again; had their meeting been arranged, or was it fortuitous? And what was their business together?

He strained his ears to try and catch some of what was passing between them, but to no avail. He was not close enough, nor dare he move any nearer without betraying his presence.

After a few minutes, he decided that there was nothing to be gained by remaining where he was, and less likelihood of attracting their attention if he returned to the theatre at once, before they made a move themselves. He suited the action to the thought, gliding silently back by the way he had come.

He entered the box just as quietly, resuming his seat beside Anthea. Julia flung him an impatient, scolding glance; but as the scene at present was the lively one between Sir Peter Teazle and his wife, she wasted no more time upon him. As for Anthea, after she had raised her brows inquiringly and received a nod promising explanations to follow, she also gave her attention to the play.

At the next interval, he briefly informed her of the meeting between Fellowes and Ross.

"Why, then, it does look as if they are in some way involved in this monstrous crime, don't you think, Justin? I know you and Watts are satisfied that Ross can't be the murderer, since Healey is so positive that she doesn't recognise his voice." She hesitated, lowering her whisper to a mere thread of sound. "I've been thinking that over — do you suppose she might have lied about it? Through fear, perhaps?"

He shook his head. "No, you're forgetting that there are other objections in the way of casting Ross in that particular role. It may be, however, that he's an accessory. But we'd best postpone this discussion for the present."

This was well advised, for the Cholmondleys' party had gathered round them again, making conversation more general. The acting was praised, especially that of Miss Campbell as Lady Teazle.

"Oddly enough, I'd a fancy as a boy to tread the boards," said Fulford, with a laugh. "Not that I ever showed any marked ability for acting, or for anything else, come to think of it! My schoolmasters evidently didn't labour under the delusion that they were nurturing a genius."

"Which of our distinguished places of learning had the privilege of educating you?" asked Justin.

"Oh, Westminster," replied Fulford, casually. "Damned stuffy place, too. Where did you go, Mr Rutherford?"

"Harrow, but the authorities endeavour to forget that fact," said Justin with a grin. "It took the masters some years to recover."

This caused general laughter, and Cholmondley launched into a monologue about his own schooldays which lasted until the interval ended.

They all returned to their seats, becoming increasingly engrossed in the play as the action accelerated, and outbursts of laughter were punctuated by tense moments when one might have heard a pin drop. Anthea sat on the edge of her chair holding her breath during the scene where Lady Teazle hides behind a screen to avoid discovery by her husband during a compromising situation.

It was over at last, the epilogue spoken by Miss Campbell, and the audience dispersing amid general enthusiasm. On the way out, a brief interchange between the Cholmondleys and their neighbours confirmed arrangements for the outing to Rievaulx on the following day.

17

ANTHEA was not the kind of female to wear her heart on her sleeve, so she appeared to be in her usual spirits; but under the facade of normality a good deal of unhappiness was concealed.

She had been taken unawares by the strength of her feelings for Rogers. She had realised that he appealed to her more than any other man she had met, and that she felt vaguely dissatisfied at their relationship being on the same light, flirtatious footing that she enjoyed with others. She had felt instinctively that she could look to him for support in moments of stress, which was the reason why she had run into his arms after her fright at the fire in the gipsy's tent at the Knavesmire.

But until he had declared his love, it had never seriously occurred to her that she, too, was in love and for the first time. Her response to his embraces had been as wholehearted as any man could desire, and in keeping with her temperament. Why, then, did she have to spoil it all by refusing to marry him at once, as he so ardently insisted? What perverse streak in her made her tempt fate so far as to risk losing him?

These were questions she asked herself time and again during the hours that followed his departure, and she could find no satisfactory answers. She only knew that, deeply as she loved him and wanted to join her life to his, there was still some unsatisfied part of herself awaiting expression. Until she had assuaged that feeling, their partnership could only be an uneasy one. What precisely it was that she needed, for the life of her she could not decide. She had told him she wished to travel overseas, visit foreign places and peoples for herself and by herself. That was part of it, certainly, although she knew well that it would be difficult to gratify this wish. No gently nurtured girl could hope to be allowed such a degree of freedom. She would be obliged to accept the escort of a male relative; and, that being so, why not that of a husband?

No, she admitted, it was more that she did not yet feel ready to settle down into the humdrum of the married state. And blissful as her senses told her marriage to Sidney would be at first, there was no escaping the melancholy fact that couples *did* settle down to become humdrum. Mayhap later on she would be ready to pay the price — but not yet.

Having reached this conclusion, she made a determined effort to put an end to the vexing internal debate, and concentrate instead on what was going forward around her. The visit to the theatre gave a new turn to her thoughts, and then there was the outing to Rievaulx on the following day.

She was keenly interested in Justin's investigation into the murder, and eager to assist in any possible way. For some days she had been looking for an opportunity to try and glean from Mrs Cholmondley some information about that lady's guests; now one suddenly appeared.

The two parties were to make the journey in an assemblage of vehicles — two chaises and three curricles. The Firsdale Hall chaise held Julia, Louisa, Anthea and the two younger girls, for Mrs de Ryde had yielded to her sister-in-law's persuasion to permit Anne to go. The other was occupied solely by Mr and Mrs Cholmondley.

"And I declare it's absurd, dear Lady Marton, that you should be so monstrously crushed!" exclaimed Mrs Cholmondley. "Even though Miss Fanny and her little friend do not take up much space, you will all be a deal more comfortable, I'm sure, if one of the young ladies were to travel in our chaise — or even two of them, if they don't wish to be parted. Now, what do you say, ma'am?"

"Why, I will be most happy to accept," put in Anthea, quickly, before Julia could open her lips to reply. "It is vastly kind of you, ma'am, and will certainly add to the comfort of the journey."

Justin, who was driving Harry in his curricle, darted her an appreciative glance, and forestalled Fulford in assisting

Anthea to make the change.

Fulford was driving Barnet in his curricle, while Fellowes had taken up Reade, neither of the two passengers having brought a conveyance to York.

The day was fine, but fortunately not too hot. This was a boon to Anthea, as she always tended to feel the stuffiness of a chaise, much preferring an open carriage. However, there had been nothing for it today but to make the journey in that way. Had Sprog been there . . . but there was no benefit in thinking of that.

The procession moved off, and Mrs Cholmondley's tongue likewise went into motion. For some time, Anthea listened politely to her inanities, putting in a word here and there, awaiting her chance to turn the conversation into more rewarding channels. The lady's husband, after a good natured attempt to give their passenger a larger share in the conversation, at length fell silent, and was presently seen to nod. Mrs Cholmondley gave Anthea a knowing smile and lowered her voice.

"It's the motion, my dear. He nearly

always drops off on a coach journey. No matter — we may still go on talking quietly together. That was another reason why I thought it would be agreeable to have you travel with us — that, and the fact that five people in a coach does make it a trifle cramped, of course. But it is pleasant to have company, is it not? Especially female company — not that I don't find our gentlemen guests agreeable, quite the reverse, for they are all delightful, I assure you!"

"Doubtless you and your husband will miss them when they return home," answered Anthea, seizing quickly on this lead. "Do you know where they live, ma'am? I believe Mr Fellowes said his home was near Whitby, and Mr Reade mentioned the Midlands without naming a particular town. But I expect you will have heard all about them by this time — their homes, their families, all the little interesting things which we females delight in knowing."

Mrs Cholmondley beamed on her.

"Yes, we do, do we not, my dear, and I can't think why some people condemn such harmless chat as gossip, can you?

Well, as to Mr Reade, his home is somewhere west of Birmingham — he mentioned the Clent hills once, though I know nothing of that country myself. But he has precious little to say of his family, if indeed he has one — I don't even know whether or not he is married. I think he spends most of his time away from home, in any case, travelling around to various sporting events."

Anthea made a polite murmur, but judged it wiser to say nothing that would interrupt.

"Mr Fellowes, as you say, has a residence near Whitby, though I collect he also spends much of his time in London. He once let slip that he has a wife, though I could discover nothing of the lady, nor of any family. You may be sure I would try, my dear Miss Rutherford, and can you blame me?"

"Indeed, no," agreed Anthea, twinkling. "I have the liveliest curiosity myself! But your gentlemen do not sound vastly communicative about their personal concerns, ma'am, although I think in general that is a fault of the male sex.

Are the other two gentlemen any more rewarding?"

To her annoyance, at that moment the chaise pulled in to the inn at Hovingham for a change of horses, thus putting an end to a most promising conversation. Mr Cholmondley awoke, and they all alighted from their separate vehicles and entered the inn to partake of coffee.

"I see your friend Mr Rogers is not with your party today," said Barnet to Anthea, as they chanced to come together on entering the coffee room. "Not an indisposition, I trust?"

She did not like the reference to 'her friend', but bit back the retort that rose to her lips.

"Oh, no, merely a business engagement elsewhere," she replied, airily. "Did you enjoy the play yesterday evening, sir?"

"Certainly. Miss Campbell gave an excellent performance."

"What did you think of the others?"

He pursed up his lips. "Some good — some not so good. A few, perhaps, bad."

"You are very severe. Do you take a keen interest in the drama, Mr Barnet?"

"I can tell you positively that he does not," put in Fulford, edging his way between them. "Didn't you hear him admitting yesterday evening that he hadn't attended the theatre since I don't know when?"

"I believe you, too, Sir John, made the same shameful admission," retorted Anthea, with a saucy look.

"Ah, yes, but one can't be doing everything, y'know, Miss Anthea, and what with race meetings, not to mention balls and parties, which I dare swear are more to your taste — "

"Do you attend the London balls, sir? That's to say, if you chance to have a house in Town?"

"I'm there now and then," he replied, evasively. "I'm by way of being a nomad, y'know, ma'am. Indeed, I think all four of us are." He glanced about him at the others, who were dispersing to seat themselves at one or other of the small tables in the room. "But pray be seated, Miss Anthea. Here is a convenient chair."

He put a hand under her arm to guide her to the nearest vacant place, but she gently moved away from it.

"I see my aunt has saved me a place at her table, and is beckoning to me to join them. Pray forgive me, Sir John."

She smiled disarmingly at him as she turned aside to join her family. Fulford sat down beside Barnet.

Barnet gave him a quizzical look.

"I fear you'll never make a conquest there, my dear chap."

"Y'know, Barnet, you've got a devilish nasty tongue at times! D'you think you'd fare any better yourself?"

Barnet's thin face took on a bleak expression for a moment in contrast to his usual nonchalant look.

"Oh, no, but then I never try my luck with any but ladybirds."

Fulford looked at him curiously. "Ever been wed, Barnet?"

The other shook his head. "Know when I'm well off."

Fulford shrugged. "You're in the right of it. I was, once. Not a success — we parted."

He seemed to regret having said so much, and at once switched the conversation to horseflesh, praising the pair which Justin was driving that day.

As Justin had just joined them along with Harry, he was able to benefit from these compliments. Having very sharp ears, however, he had managed to overhear most of the couple's previous remarks.

The party did not linger very long over their coffee interval, but soon were on their way again. To Anthea's secret annoyance, it was some time before she was able to learn any more about the Cholmondleys' guests. Mr Cholmondley seemed to be much more lively after the break in their journey, and joined his spouse in keeping up a running commentary on the countryside through which they were passing, and every other topic which occurred to either of them.

They were within a few miles of Helmsley, where they had bespoken a luncheon at the ancient Black Swan, before Cholmondley fell silent and closed his eyes once more.

In desperation, Anthea attempted to turn the conversation back to the point at which it had been abandoned.

"You were telling me, ma'am, before we stopped for coffee, about your gentlemen guests," she said, abruptly, interrupting Mrs Cholmondley in the middle of something else.

The lady looked surprised, but only for a moment. Perhaps she was used to being interrupted, as chatterboxes are.

"Oh, yes, but I must just finish telling you about this new modiste's in the town, my dear, for you may wish to visit her yourself — although, of course, I do realise that London shops must be far superior to most, I think you'll agree that this one is something quite out of the common way . . . "

It continued for another ten minutes or so, and Anthea was quite in a ferment. She foresaw little opportunity for the remainder of the day to have Mrs Cholmondley to herself. Once arrived at Helmsley, they would be mingled among the rest of the party, with small chance of any private conversation.

Perhaps the older woman sensed that she had lost her companion's attention, although Anthea continued to listen with a fixed, bright smile and to make the right responses. Presently, the anecdote ceased.

"Yes, well, you were saying, Miss

Anthea, that gentlemen do not talk very much about personal matters, and I think that is all too true in most instances. For all I have learnt about most of my guests, they might be deaf and dumb! That is to say, of course, they do talk a deal, but always about such topics as gentlemen enjoy, and never those interesting, intimate little details which we females do like to hear about other people's lives! But one of them, at least, has told me something of his home and family, and that is Mr Barnet. It seems he has a mother living somewhere in Sussex, and he spends part of his time with her and part in bachelor accommodation in London."

Anthea felt somewhat surprised at this news; Mr Barnet did not strike her as a devoted son, tied to his mother's apron strings.

"What part of Sussex, ma'am?" she asked, casually.

"He's never said, although I rather think I did once ask, but I may be mistaken. I did not gain the impression that there was a family seat, however, but a more modest kind of residence.

Nor do I have the least notion whether he has any other family — brothers and sisters and so on — but I believe I've heard him tell one of the others that he's not married. As for Sir John Fulford, try as I will I can get nothing out of him except that he goes around the country to all the sporting events, which I believe is true of all our guests! He seems to be familiar with London, and I've heard him mention Brighton as a town he frequents, besides I don't know how many towns with racecourses — there's no end to the list! But no mention of a home."

"I know that Mr Reade and Mr Barnet were chance met acquaintances, ma'am, but how did your husband come to invite the others to your home for the Races?"

"Oh, they were just as chance met, my dear — my husband does not stand on ceremony, you know. I believe it may have been at Doncaster or one of those other racecourses where he fell in with them, and heard they were coming to York, so offered them hospitality."

"I collect the two gentlemen were already acquainted with each other when

Mr Cholmondley met them?"

"Oh, no, no such thing!" declared Mrs Cholmondley, emphatically. "Indeed, I am persuaded that they do not like each other above half. Mr Fellowes is vastly different from Sir John, you know — the one so staid, while the other — dear me, you must have noticed — a prodigious flirt!"

Anthea agreed that she had noticed this.

"Sir John and Mr Barnet seem to go along together tolerably — they are always off somewhere together, especially in the evenings. The other two are more inclined to solitary pursuits, although Mr Barnet often takes an afternoon stroll on his own, too. But, of course, my husband sees to it that they all make up a party for the most of their outings — it is so vastly agreeable to be all together, is it not? Just as we are today, thanks to your aunt's kind suggestion!"

Although her companion continued to chat away, Anthea found she did not learn any more on the only subject of interest to her; so she was not sorry when they all alighted at Helmsley for their luncheon at the Black Swan.

After an excellent meal, they strolled about the picturesque little market town with its impressive castle. The four storey keep with turrets and battlements above, and the fine earthworks surrounding the ruins fascinated Justin, and he determined to make another visit there alone, when he would have leisure to do justice to it. At the moment, no one showed as keen an interest in the castle as himself, all being intent on pressing forward for Rievaulx, a matter of a further three miles.

* * *

"'Pon my word, I don't know when I saw a finer abbey!" exclaimed Reade.

They were walking high up along the grass terrace at Rievaulx, with the Abbey below, seen in changing aspects through the viewing channels cut among the trees surrounding the terrace.

"Then you've never seen Fountains," declared Julia. "That is certainly the most magnificent of them all, Mr Reade, and I trust you'll have time to pay a visit there before you leave our part of the country."

"Don't suppose I'll be staying much longer, Lady Marton. Race week's over, and I don't feel I can trespass further on Mr and Mrs Cholmondley's hospitality."

This brought a spirited rebuttal from both these good people.

"Y'know what," said Fulford to Justin in an aside, "they're too damned hospitable! Easiest thing in the world for anyone to take advantage of 'em!"

"Yes, I can quite see that. In fact, one does wonder if possibly at some time or other they'll harbour a wrong 'un," returned Justin.

Fulford gave him a sidelong glance.

"Any particular reason for saying that?"

"Not the least in the world, my dear chap. What I really meant was that, with such a casual way of making up their house parties, they might now and then find some are ill-assorted." Justin made the glib reply in convincing tones. "Tell me, how do you go along with your fellow guests?"

Fulford shrugged. They were a little apart from the others at present, so could not be overheard.

"They're a good enough set of fellows. One learns to take men as one finds them, from schooldays on."

"After Westminster, Oxford or Cambridge?" asked Justin, casually.

There was the slighted hesitation before Fulford made his reply.

"Neither," he admitted. "Wasn't an academic, so m'father felt it was a waste to send me to university. Had a year or two at home, then took the Grand Tour."

"Home being somewhere other than Yorkshire, I collect?"

For a moment, Fulford regarded him suspiciously, and Justin wondered whether he was doing it too brown.

"As you say," was the cryptic reply.

Justin smoothly switched the conversation to the Grand Tour, a subject which brought contributions from several members of the party, notably the voluble Cholmondley. Only Barnet and Reade were silent; perhaps, reflected Justin, through lack of interest.

Presently they reached the Ionic Temple, which was furnished as a dining room for al fresco meals by the Duncombe family. Here a footman and housemaid welcomed them with refreshments.

"I declare," said Anthea to Louisa, "it will take me quite a fortnight to recover from this orgy of eating and drinking! Do I look at all *bloated* to you, Louisa?"

"My dear young lady," remarked Fulford, with an ingratiating leer, "you look as utterly charming as always, I assure you!"

"Thank you, but I don't feel it."

She turned away from him to converse in a lower tone to her cousin, evidently wishing to exclude him. Barnet gave him another of his cynical looks, and Fulford scowled.

"What a delightful ornamental temple this is!" enthused Mrs Cholmondley. "Everything of the first style of elegance, and in just as perfect order as any dining room in a commodious residence!"

"Very true, ma'am," agreed Justin, glancing around the table at which they were all seated and raising his voice slightly so that all could hear. "Perfect order, indeed — I dare say there isn't a loose tile in the place."

Several of the party laughed. As he

had anticipated, the remark brought a conscious look to the faces of Fanny and Anne de Ryde, and a momentary flicker of surprise to Anthea's.

But as he had hoped, there was one other present who also registered, albeit fleetingly, the same emotion.

18

THE party returned from the outing to Rievaulx pleasurably tired and looking forward to a relaxing evening spent in their separate homes.

Not so Justin, who slipped out after dinner for an arranged meeting with Watts in the privacy of the landlord's snug private parlour at the Black Horse.

"I may as well tell you straight away, Joe," began Justin, a tankard of home brewed in his hand, "that I think I know who the culprit is."

"Well, that's good news, guv'nor!" Watts gave him a shrewd look. "But when you say that ye *think* ye know — "

"That's the devil of it. It's a strong suspicion, but it only rests on a fleeting expression I caught on his face. We were all seated in an ornamental temple at the time, and I said that there wouldn't be any loose tiles there."

"Crafty," approved the Runner.

"Well, yes, I didn't think it too bad on the spur of the moment," admitted Justin with a grin. "But, damme, Joe, it's only a pointer, not evidence, and moreover one could easily be mistaken, so I don't propose to give you his name as yet. I managed to gather some particulars about the antecedents of these four men — with the invaluable aid of my niece, I hasten to add."

"Ah, yes, she's a right one, is Miss Rutherford, if ye'll pardon the liberty, sir. Are ye wishful to inform me of these particulars, or shall I give you my findings first? Not that they amount to more'n a couple of brass farthings."

"A pity. Never mind, you tell me first."

"As ye've said already, guv'nor, I think we can set our sights on these four gennelmen up at Warton Manor, for I've now looked into the affairs of the other parties new to the district, and they're harmless enough. All except that Ross, o' course, and even if he 'bain't a murderer and an ex-convict, he's a wrong 'un, right enough, and I'll catch him, see if I don't. Anyways, not to make a long tale of it, I took y'r suggestion, sir, and had a nice, quiet look round at their rooms while they were out today."

Justin nodded approvingly. "With the assistance of the little parlourmaid, I presume? I hope you made it worth her while, Joe."

"Nay, I'd no need to bring the moll into it. I knew where the bedchambers were already from information received — " he grinned — "and there was no one to speak of about, as the servants had decided to have a day out, too. What's sauce for the goose, sir! I just slipped up there by the back stairs, and the only fly in the ointment was that tarnation valet who works for Mr Fellowes. He was hanging around his master's bedchamber most of the time I was upstairs, so I had to wait on my chance to get into it. Howsomever, he did pop off downstairs for a few minutes at last. I was keeping close watch so was able to slip in quickly. Daren't stay long, but long enough to see that he'd been busy packing all his master's effects — clean as a whistle, all drawers, cupboards, the closet, and such like, except for a set of evening togs laid out on the bed! Puzzled me, I don't mind admitting. What d'ye reckon, guv'nor? Is he set to do a moonlit flit?"

Justin frowned thoughtfully and set down his tankard.

"This queers my pitch, Joe, as I think you'd say. I'd thought this man Fellowes an unlikely starter for our villain, as everything I've managed to learn of him suggests that he can't possibly have been out of the country for the past fourteen years or more. He may be lying through his teeth, of course, but he can't have had much time to find out such details concerning the theatre, for example, as he appears to know. Certainly the other three men weren't as well informed. Then there's the valet, and the connection with Ross. Difficult, if not impossible, to strike up a close acquaintance with either in such a short space of time. And what inducement could he offer them to participate in a plot designed solely for vengeance? Money? He may, of course, have resources hidden away sufficient for that."

He brooded a moment, rumpling his hair in the gesture well known to Watts.

Then he gave a sudden exclamation.

"Got it! At least, I think I have! If so, old chap, you're in for double trouble!"

He explained, while his companion listened and then nodded.

"Ay, that's very likely, sir. Wonder we didn't think of it afore. So I'll do a spell of surveillance later on — reckon he won't move until well after midnight, if he does at all, say one or two o'clock onwards — that's if we've guessed aright."

"And I'll join you — that's settled. Now, tell me what you found in the rooms of the other three men."

"Precious little, beside togs — clothes, that's to say. Sir John Fulford had a few bills lying about, but no letters, nothing of a personal nature. There was a copy of *The Gentleman's Magazine* with an advertisement of a horse for sale that he'd ringed round. Y'know guv'nor, the usual thing 'sweet goer, strong well rounded quarters' and so on. Don't think that tells us much, do you?"

"Unless it gave the advertiser's home direction, and not just that of the journal?"

"Ah, yes, it did, sir, in this case, so I

copied it down to be on the safe side. Here we are."

He produced his notebook and flicked over a page. Justin scanned the few lines.

"A Mr Charles Meyer, and a house in Brighton. Well, by what we've learnt of Fulford, he's familiar with both Brighton and London. A letter to this gentleman asking if Fulford did indeed purchase the animal might disclose where Fulford lives. On the other hand, if Meyer was never approached by him, we'll be no further forward. But it's worth trying — I'll send a letter off by first post tomorrow. So much for Fulford — now what of the other two?"

"Mr Reade had Lud knows how many racing journals, but nothing of a personal nature, unless ye count a silver brush set with the initials AR on each piece."

"Fairly new, was it?" asked Justin, with a glimmer of interest.

"Not old, at any rate — could have been purchased recently, I dare say. I see what ye're thinking, guv'nor," he added.

Justin nodded. "And Barnet?"

"Didn't have much of anything."

"I was hoping there might have been a letter from his mother."

"Lud, is he a mother's lad?" Watts asked cynically.

"Don't know that, but my niece learnt that he lives with his mother somewhere in Sussex. I had hoped she'd have written to him while he's here, so that we'd have his direction at home."

"No such luck, sir, nor with t'other gent, Mr Reade. That one's got a mort of boots, sir — boots for walking and riding, enough to equip a small army!"

"Has he so? Y'know, Joe, he's the one we know least about, come to think of it, because he disclaims all interest in any subject other than sporting pursuits. Said he didn't care a button for the theatre — could cover ignorance of fourteen years' standing, don't you think? After all, what do we know of others but that which they choose to tell us? And anyone with the least wit can fabricate a sufficiently convincing tale."

"True, guv'nor. But it's our job to find proof, and that we'll do, come hell or high water," Watts averred. "I'll be on watch tonight, and may need to call on you."

"Like old times in the Peninsula, eh, Joe? Miss them sometimes, I must admit. Yes, you can rely on me."

* * *

At a little after three o'clock in the morning, all was dark and silent at Warton Manor. A door opened quietly on the upstairs landing, and two figures stealthily emerged. Both were carrying luggage; one held a dark lantern with part of a shutter opened to provide a faint light. They started to descend the stairs, carefully testing each one as they trod, to avoid the danger of a squeak.

Stealthy as they were, it seemed that someone had been alerted. A neighbouring door opened the slightest crack, and an unseen pair of eyes observed them for a matter of seconds before the door was closed again.

They saw nothing of this; their backs were towards the landing and the meagre light they carried was focused on the way ahead. Having descended yet another flight of stairs, they came to the kitchen, where a faint glow was given off by a fire banked down for the night. They crossed the floor to the back door, quietly unlocking it and drawing back the bolts. Emerging into the yard where the pump stood, they hurried across it to make their way to the stables and the exit into a lane beyond.

A curricle was waiting for them here with a pair, harnessed to it. A man was walking the horses to keep them quiet. A few brief words were exchanged, the luggage swiftly strapped on to the back of the vehicle, and the couple climbed into it, one of them taking up the reins. The man with the horses walked a few yards down the lane to where another horse was tethered. He mounted, and prepared to follow the curricle.

Watts and Justin had been keeping watch in the kitchen garden from one of the small greenhouses which overlooked the path to the stables. The moon was riding high behind a barrier of cloud and seldom put in an appearance; but there was just sufficient light for their eyes, accustomed now to the darkness, to discern the two moving forms with their burdens.

They left their shelter and followed at a discreet distance, taking cover whenever their quarry slackened pace. They waited a while before moving out into the lane; but presently they heard the clop of hoofs and the jingle of horses' harness, and knew that the fugitives were moving away.

It was then that they saw the third man following the curricle on horseback.

"As we supposed," whispered Justin, "our friend Ross, no less. He had the curricle waiting for them. So to horse, my friend! But softly does it — at this hour, every hoofbeat will sound like a clarion call unless we keep to the fields. We may be tolerably certain of their destination, wouldn't you say?"

"Ay, no doubt of it, guv'nor — York, and First Water Lane into the bargain. Lie up there until close on time for a coach to leave for — London, would ye say? Best place to get rid o' the loot — and to hide away for a spell, too."

They sprinted back to the spot in the grounds where they had left two horses ready and waiting, and were quickly off in pursuit. Once they reached the turnpike road, they kept to the fields beside it, as there was no other traffic abroad; but soon they entered the town, where haycarts and waggons from the country, together with the occasional horseman, offered them plenty of cover.

It was evident that they had guessed right, for the three fugitives made for First Water Lane, eventually entering the house where Watts had seen Fellowes go on a previous occasion. The curricle had first been driven into the yard of the alehouse next door, and left there together with the horse ridden by Ross. A fourth man had admitted them to the house.

By now the first streaks of dawn were in the clouded sky, but it was still dark.

"Keep watch, Joe," murmured Justin. "I'll stable the nags, then go to the nearest Justice for a warrant. The London coach leaves the Black Swan at five o'clock, and it's now a quarter to four, so we've ample time — that's if our reckoning's not amiss."

Watts grinned as he dismounted, handing his horse's rein to Justin.

"Reckon the Justice won't welcome ye at this hour, guv'nor!"

"Precisely why I came — he might refuse to rise from his bed even for a Bow Street man, but will scarcely deny the representative of another Yorkshire Justice."

The morning air was a trifle raw, and Watts was missing his sleep. He paced up and down quietly, keeping one eye on his objective meanwhile, but shivering a little at times. No sound or movement came from the house or from the street, until the dawn came up reluctantly. Then one or two people emerged from the neglected dwellings — a sweep with his brushes, a costermonger with his barrow — giving signs of a new day beginning. They glanced incuriously at Watts, too wary to concern themselves with others in a street where curiosity did not pay dividends.

Watts had not long to wait. In about twenty minutes, Justin appeared with two burly constables at his heels. He handed the search warrant to Watts.

They approached the house, and Watts banged upon the door. Justin motioned to one of the constables to follow him round to the back of the house. They reached it just as Watts gave another resounding thump on the front door, accompanied by a shout.

"Open in the King's name!"

Receiving no response, the Runner and his constable put their shoulders to the door. The rotting wood gave readily, and they charged into the room beyond.

The four occupants had already run through into the tiny scullery to the rear door. One of them wrenched it open, but started back in dismay as he saw the two men awaiting him outside. He started to pull a pistol from his coat, but Justin moved in swiftly, gripping his wrist.

"I'll have that, I think, Fellowes," he said.

Watts grinned as he handcuffed the prisoners.

* * *

Justin arrived back at Firsdale Hall shortly after ten o'clock. Early as the hour was for social calls, he found Cholmondley closeted with his brother-in-law.

Both greeted him with grave faces.

"Don't know where y've been, Justin. None of my business," said Sir George. "Only Cholmondley here's come to report the most devilish thing to me! All his wife's jewellery and some of the family silver stolen overnight! And what's more, that chap Fellowes and his valet have disappeared without leaving a stitch behind — curricle gone, as well! Onc can't help but draw the conclusion that Fellowes must be responsible and the valet an accessory. I'll have to question the servants at the Manor, of course, but — "

"No need," interrupted Justin, having greeted the distracted Cholmondley. "I know all about it. Watts is with one of the York magistrates now. He's arrested Fellowes, the valet and your groom Ross — " Sir George started — "yes, you'll find Ross has decamped, too. He was one of the gang of jewel thieves led by the man Fellowes — if that's his real name. But no need to disturb yourself, Mr Cholmondley, for all your stolen property is safe. You've but to go into York to identify it, and then you may bring it safely home."

Cholmondley exclaimed in relief at this news, and for the next half hour or so was vociferous with questions and thanks. Justin satisfied him as best he could without revealing the real reason why he and Watts had been keeping an eye on the guests at Warton Manor.

"But a man who was my guest," said Cholmondley mournfully, "a gentleman, as I thought! I declare it shakes one's faith in human nature! How can I tell my dear wife?"

"I imagine she will be overcome with joy at the recovery of her jewels," remarked Justin, drily, "and every other matter will fade into insignificance. Tell me, sir, where and when did you meet this man and invite him to your home for Races week?"

Cholmondley made an effort to pull himself together, for he was considerably flustered.

"I'm not quite sure — now, would it have been at the Knayesmire during the spring races? I think it was! He'd come specially for the meetings, and chanced to mention that he meant to come again in August, and of course I said I'd be happy to put him up, and so it was arranged. Much pleasanter than trying to book in at an hotel, as I'm sure you'll agree, Rutherford, and of course my wife and I simply delight in company!"

"You can't recall if anyone of your acquaintance introduced this man to you?"

Cholmondley shook his head. "No, we just fell into conversation in the way one does."

Justin and Sir George exchanged glances.

"Possibly, my dear chap," said the latter, "you may find it wiser for the future to know rather more about chance-met acquaintances before inviting them into your home. However, this matter hasn't turned out too badly, as luck will have it."

He turned to Justin.

"I suppose Runner Watts to be delayed in York giving evidence to the magistrates? No doubt he'll have more to tell us on his return. Were these three men responsible for the general outbreak of robberies in this area of late, d'ye know, Justin?"

"As it happens, I do. They were all clapped into gaol after Watts arrested them, and hauled before the magistrates about eight o'clock. The fourth member of the gang — the one who rented the dwelling in First Water Lane — couldn't peach on the rest fast enough! Said they'd threatened his life if he didn't let them use his place for their nefarious ends, and so forth. He was the fellow whom Watts saw meeting Ross at a coffee house in York, by the way — told you of that, George, you remember?"

"A vastly pretty little scheme they'd worked out," said Sir George. "Two men in the house posing as master and servant, a third working in a nearby stables, and a 'flash house', as they call 'em, only a few miles off in the city! I'd give a deal to know how often they've worked that trick! Well, they won't do so again, I'll warrant — they'll be up for trial at the next Assizes, meantime they'll rest in gaol. I dare say your man Runner Watts won't lose by bringing this affair to a successful conclusion," he added.

"No, indeed!" exclaimed Cholmondley. "I and my dear spouse can't be sufficiently grateful to him, I'm sure! And we shall certainly express that gratitude in practical terms! Only to think — all is recovered! I must hasten home to acquaint my dearest Maria with the welcome tidings!"

19

LIFE at Denby House was slowly returning to normal after the recent catastrophic events. Philip de Ryde would be immobilised for some time to come, but his general health was good, and the concussion had left no permanent damage. His daughter Anne looked in to his room every day to cheer him up and play an occasional game of backgammon; neither were his neighbours lacking in all those attentions which help to alleviate a patient's boredom.

Under the sensible administration of his sister Cassandra de Ryde, domestic affairs were comfortable again, while the influence of the de Rydes' old nurse had restored even the mistress of the house to a less tragic frame of mind. She began to interest herself tentatively in the embroidery of which she had once been fond, and Nurse encouraged this.

On the morning of those events which Justin was even then discussing with Sir

George and Cholmondley, and of which the inhabitants of the village were so far ignorant, Mrs de Ryde sent Healey down to the village shop.

"I need some silk of this colour, Healey — " handing the maid a strand of deep blue — "but don't on any account bring it if it's not the exact shade, for that will ruin all. I don't trust that female in Wilson's — don't let her persuade you, mind! If she hasn't got it, then you must go into York for it, only that means so much delay."

Healey promised to be careful in her choice, and set out on her errand. She, too, was feeling somewhat restored after all her tribulations. There had been no more sinister messages since the one leading to her master's accident; better still, she had not set eyes on that dreaded monster. And although her interview with Sir George Marton on Sunday had been terrifying enough to scare the living daylights out of a body, in the end he had been tolerant, and not meted out to her the punishment she had feared.

The village was only half a mile distant from Denby House. It boasted three or four small shops. There was Ned Appleton's general store, which was also the mail receiving office, a butcher's, a baker's, and Mr Wilson's emporium, as it was grandiloquently named, where one could buy haberdashery and certain small items of female dress.

Healey permitted herself a lingering gaze in the window before entering the shop. She had all the feminine love of pretty things, and though Wilson's offered only a meagre display, it was better than nothing.

She was gazing in rapt attention at an embroidered reticule which she rather fancied, when suddenly male voices intruded on her reverie. She looked round quickly.

Three men were striding past her in the direction of the Black Horse, talking together in low tones. One voice rose suddenly above the rest.

"And I say it's as plain as the nose on your face! Fellowes lifted the loot — who else? And why else d'ye suppose he and that valet of his vanished overnight? Besides, I saw 'em go."

Her heart seemed to stop beating

altogether as sheer terror flooded her. That voice! She knew it, could not possibly mistake it! Had it not taunted her on that dreadful night in the temple at Denby House?

Her wild eyes remained fixed for a moment on the speaker, like those of a mesmerised rabbit. He noticed her, and a flicker of recognition passed over his face. It was gone in a moment as the cold, hard eyes turned away from her. But she realised that the die was cast.

She knew him — and he knew that she knew.

What should she do?

She stood still for several minutes, frozen by panic. Gradually her mind began to work again, although slowly. She recalled another voice, that of the Justice, Sir George Marton, saying to her, "You must give us all the assistance you can to uncover this murderer."

Yes, yes, she would — not only to save herself from the punishment of the law, but from the far worse retribution which awaited her at the hands of this madman! If only she could reach someone in time, before Pringle could stop her mouth, as he would surely do now that he had seen she recognised him! Who? Sir George Marton? But he might be from home, and she must not take too long over her errand, for fear the mistress would be angry and turn her off for good. This had been hinted at several times of late, when Healey had been in a fit of nervous depression. She wrung her hands. Dear God, there were so many hazards, she did not for the life of her know which to concentrate upon.

Then it came to her. The Bow Street Runner — was he not lodging at the Black Horse at present? If only those three men might not be going there, too . . .

She looked after them down the street, and saw that they had gone past the inn. Screwing her courage to the sticking point, she forced her shaky legs to walk on to her objective. She reached it and pushed open the taproom door.

To her relief, there were no customers within at that early hour, only the landlord polishing some glasses. He paused at sight of her, surprised.

"Mrs Healey, good morning, ma'am.

Can I get tha owt?"

"No, no thank ye," she stammered. "I came to see — " she swallowed — "Mr Watts. Is he in?"

He eyed her curiously before shaking his head.

"Nay, that he's not."

He refrained from adding that his guest had not been in all night, thinking that it was wiser to keep silent on that point, Watts being a Bow Street officer.

She looked dismayed, clutching the counter as if in need of support.

"When — when will he be back, d'you know?" she asked tremulously.

He shook his head. "No notion, ma'am. Can I tak' a message, sithee?"

She hesitated. She dared not say much, yet feared to waste any time in making contact with Watts.

"Tell him I must see him at once — it's urgent!" she said at last, in shaking tones. "Tell him to come to the servants' entrance at Denby House and I'll be looking out for him — but don't delay, will you? Let him know *at once*, as soon as you see him!"

"Ay, never fret, Mrs Healey, I'll tell

him," the landlord said, soothingly. "Summat's upset 'ee, I can see."

Perhaps he hoped that she would confide in him, but such a course never entered her head. She nodded her thanks and turned to run out of the inn 'like one possessed', as he told Watts not very much later.

She barely retained control of her wits sufficiently to conclude the errand on which she had been sent and return to the house. After delivering the embroidery silk to her mistress, she begged leave to stroll out of doors for a while as she had the headache.

Madam had much to say on the subject of maids who gave themselves airs and fancied they had the megrims; but as Nanny was sitting with her, she was content to allow Healey to go.

At once the maid hurried downstairs to the servants' entrance avoiding the rest of the staff; and, closing the door behind her, began to pace up and down the paths through the kitchen gardens. Anxiety drove her so that she could not be still for a moment.

She had been there for almost an hour

when a little lad approached her. Vaguely she recognised him as the youngest of the gardeners' boys.

"Please 'm, there's a man axin' for 'ee," he piped, nervously.

She started. "Where? Who?"

He looked even more nervous. "At t'back door into t'lane, 'm — " he gestured in the direction of a path leading beyond the stables to a lane beside the boundary wall of the house. "Says to tell 'ee it's Maister Watts, 'm, please 'm."

She made an inarticulate sound and bounded away like a startled deer. The boy stared after her for a moment, then ran off towards the house.

She continued on her way, now running, now walking breathlessly. She skirted the stables, not wishing to encounter the grooms, and soon reached her objective, panting and dishevelled but with a strong surge of relief.

This vanished for a moment as she saw to her disappointment that no one was there. Then confidence flooded back; of course, he would be outside, waiting for her in the lane. Why, she was not clear, but she accepted that a Bow Street man would have his own way of going about things.

She lifted the latch and stepped out into the lane, which was deserted save for one man and a horse tethered nearby.

Yes, he was there.

But *not* the man she had rushed hopefully to meet. This was the threatening monster of her nightmares.

She threw back her head and screamed at the top of her lungs before his steel grip tightened about her throat.

* * *

When the three visitors returned to Warton Manor after their morning stroll, they were greeted enthusiastically by their host, not long returned from his call on Sir George. Both Mr and Mrs Cholmondley lost no time in acquainting them with the happy state of affairs which was to restore the family valuables almost as soon as they were lost. In their joy at this outcome, both husband and wife seemed to lose sight of the unpleasant fact that they had, so to speak, nourished a viper in their bosom.

Their three guests, however, showed signs of uneasiness.

"Damnable business for you and your lady wife, sir," commiserated Fulford. "Under the circumstances, we're sure you'll want to be quit of us as soon as possible."

Both husband and wife protested that nothing was further from their thoughts, and they would be only too happy for their visitors to remain indefinitely.

"Very good of you, Cholmondley," said Barnet, "but we've all been talking of moving on for some days now, since Race week's over. We can never be sufficiently grateful for your splendid hospitality, but as Fulford says, you can do better without guests just at present."

"Yes, indeed, ma'am," put in Reade, bowing towards Mrs Cholmondley. "The least we can do is to remove ourselves promptly."

"But you'll scarce go today!" exclaimed Cholmondley. "Why not leave it until the morning, and make an early start?"

All three appeared determined upon quitting the Manor at once, however.

"I'm going only as far as Hull for the present," announced Fulford. "I'm promised to friends there." He turned to the other two. "Either of you like a lift into York in my curricle? Might be a trifle short of luggage space, of course."

"No, no!" protested their host. "As Reade and Barnet didn't bring vehicles of their own here, my coachman shall drive them into town, if such is their wish, and they may take a post chaise from whichever of the inns they choose. Only say when you wish the coach to be ready, gentlemen — not but what I think it a great shame that you must be off!. However, perhaps you will honour us with your company on another occasion."

* * *

It was not far short of eleven o'clock when Watts rode into Firsdale village. He had been in conference with the York magistrates for some time after Justin left, and had learnt a good deal more about the robbers and their methods. He had made his deposition, and would be called upon to give evidence later at the trial of the miscreants.

Satisfactory, very, he reflected, as he stabled the horse at the back of the village inn, especially as the reward looked like being handsome. Yet, in spite of all, some feeling of dissatisfaction hung about him; he and the captain (Watts often called Justin by his erstwhile rank when communing with himself) had not yet caught the villain who had murdered Knowle and tried to kill two others.

He strode out of the inn yard, prepared to go up to the Hall and give Sir George and Justin an account of his dealings with the magistrates, when the landlord spied him and called his name. Watts turned back.

"Ye wanted me, landlord?"

"Yes, I'm glad I caught 'ee. That lady's maid at Denby House, Healey she's called — "

The Runner's glance sharpened.

"I know the wench — what about her?"

"Came into t'tap more'n half an hour agone," said Perkin. "Wanted to see 'ee, seemed in a rare talkin' when I said tha wasn't 'ere, seemed like one possessed, I reckon. Said to tell 'ee as she must see 'ee urgent like. She'll be lookin' out for 'ee at servants' entrance, but tha must go there at once, no delay, she said."

"Female fidgets, most like," replied Watts. "Ye know how it is with 'em! All the same, I'll go up there — thankee, Perkin."

As he strode away from the village, he reflected that it might be as well to take the captain along with him. If by any lucky chance the wench had news of the murderer, it would save time if they learned it together. It would take only ten minutes or so extra to go by way of Firsdale Hall, and they could use the back way into Denby House.

Arriving at the Hall, he sent a message in to Justin which brought the latter hastening out to him.

"What news on the Rialto?" quipped Justin, as they met. "Sir George was expecting you to come in and unburden yourself. Something amiss?"

Watts explained quickly.

"Yes, by Jove, we'd better get there with all speed," agreed Justin. "If she's in possession of the kind of knowledge we suspect, her life could be in danger if our man gets wind of it."

Until then, Watts had been only partly convinced of the urgency of his errand. Now Justin's words gave a startling reality to the situation.

Without more ado, they set off at a brisk pace across the grounds in the direction of the stables. At length they came to the door in the boundary wall which led to the lane between the two properties.

Justin flung it open. They emerged into the lane and headed for the back door to the grounds of Denby House.

As they came round the bend which concealed it from view, they saw a tethered horse and a man standing outside the door. It opened and a woman emerged.

The next moment a piercing scream rent the air.

They started to run. The man leapt forward to seize the woman's throat, cutting off her cry of terror.

So intent was he on his task that he failed to pay any attention to the others until they were upon him. Then he dropped the now senseless Healey on the ground, turning to face his attackers with an inhuman snarl of rage.

He fought like a madman, which indeed at that moment he was; but after a fierce struggle, he was felled to the ground and Watts clamped the handcuffs on his wrists.

* * *

Much later in the day, when yet another prisoner was safely lodged in the town gaol, Watts returned to give an official account of the proceedings to Sir George.

"The man at the flash house in York peached on the robbers a treat, y'r honour," he said. "He may think turning King's evidence will help save his skin, but I reckon the magistrates have other notions. He told of four robberies in this district and a couple in York itself, and there was a fair haul of loot still lying in the house." Course he wasn't receiving, y'r honour, oh, no! Stored the bundles for the gang without any notion of what they contained. A likely tale — thinks the Justices were born yesterday, seemingly."

"An illusion of which I'm sure they'll rapidly disabuse him," returned Sir George, drily. "Well, Runner Watts, there's no need to detain you further, as Mr Rutherford here can give me any information concerning the murderer. I collect you had a very rough passage in the coach conveying him to the York magistrates, even with the assistance of one of my burliest gardeners as well as that of Mr Rutherford. I congratulate you on a most successful mission, and I shall be writing forthwith to Sir Nathaniel Conant at Bow Street to acquaint him of your valuable work here."

Watts drew himself up in military style, his expression alight with satisfaction.

"Thankee, y'r honour. It's but my duty."

He turned to quit the room, giving a short bow to Justin and Anthea, who had been sitting there listening in silence.

The former followed him out of the room.

"I'll see you later at the Black Horse for a tankard, Joe," he said. "You'll be posting back to London tomorrow, I take it?"

"Ay, guv'nor. I've made my depositions, so there's nothing more to do here until the trials come up. I'll be off on the morning mail to make my report to Sir Nathaniel."

Justin nodded and the two parted, Justin re-entering the library.

"Thank God you've laid that murdering villain by the heels!" exclaimed Sir George. "Especially as there's small doubt but that he'd have had another touch at me before long. Healey, by the way, is recovering. I sent over to Denby House while you were absent with Watts in town. The medico says she'll do well enough, apart from bruises and a sore throat for a while, poor creature."

Both Justin and Anthea expressed their relief at this news.

"We owe her a debt of gratitude," continued Justin. "As soon as she was able to identify the murderer, she wasted no time in trying to inform us. I'm bound to admit that it might have taken long enough to find him out otherwise. I had a strong suspicion, but no proof. Indeed, until the evening of our visit to the theatre, suspicion was pretty evenly divided among all four of Cholmondley's guests. Watts had cleared all other newcomers to this area by then."

"When a man's such a fool as Cholmondley, asking complete strangers into his home, it's almost inevitable that some time or other he'll catch cold at it," stated Sir George. "But what fixed your suspicion upon the culprit during the visit to the theatre?"

"By then, I'd more or less ruled Fellowes out. He was up to something with Ross, that was evident, but I didn't think it was revenge. At the theatre, I deliberately steered the conversation on to topics concerning drama, particularly anything taking place in recent years — the rebuilding of Covent Garden and Drury Lane, the success of Edmund Kean, and so on. I don't need to tell you that I chose that subject because our man had been an actor in his youth. I was hoping that in some way he might betray himself — possibly because he would be the only one who had no knowledge of these events, owing to his absence overseas."

"But it wasn't so simple," put in Anthea, "because all three seemed equally ignorant on that head."

"Not quite," demurred Justin. "I gained an impression — vague, I must admit — that Fulford was not totally ignorant of the fires at the two theatres, although he'd never heard Kean's name. Not interested, I suppose. However, I did pick up a much stronger hint to the guilty party. It was when I mentioned that the new auditorium in both theatres was so much enlarged that one no longer had a sense of closeness and intimacy to the actors."

"And he said at once that it was essential for the audience to be able to see the expressions on the actors' faces," said Anthea, triumphantly.

"Precisely. That gave me my first clue, tenuous though it was. My second, amounting to a far stronger suspicion, came at Rievaulx when we were taking refreshment in the Ionic Temple there."

"I know — you made a remark about loose tiles! I may tell you that Fanny,

Anne and I were so busy trying hard not to appear to realise what you were at, that I quite failed to notice if any of the others showed a reaction."

"But he did, though for a matter of seconds only. And that's when I knew our murderer was the man who called himself Barnet."

* * *

"Well, it's all over," declared Anthea. "And I must say I trust you're grateful for the hours of boredom I've endured listening to Mrs Cholmondley in order to glean information for you!"

"Indeed I am — can you doubt it, dear niece?"

She looked at him suspiciously. "You have a vastly accomplished way of cozening people, you wretch!"

"Which you also possess. What of poor Sprog?"

She blushed.

"He's the best of fellows, Anthea," he said, gently.

"I know."

"Then — isn't there any hope for

him?" he ventured.

She hung her head. After a moment, she looked up, her fine hazel eyes bright with unshed tears.

"Yes, there is," she replied, in a low voice. "But pray, don't *urge* me, Justin — it must be in my own good time, when I am ready! I want to do so many things, first — have adventures, see strange countries — "

He nodded sympathetically. "We're alike in that, at least. I, too, don't wish to be tied down. But it's different for a female, of course. You're not the stuff of old maids, chit!"

"That may be so, but I myself will decide," she said, firmly.

"So be it. Let us hope that Sprog will wait. No, very well, I don't mean to tease you. As to seeing foreign parts, after I've browsed around here in Yorkshire among the splendid antiquities, I'm thinking of going off to visit my brother Hugh in Turkey — as you know, he's in The Diplomatic Service. Would you care to come? Suitably chaperoned on the journey, of course, as your mama will insist, though Hugh's wife can take over that responsibility when you're with them. Little the poor female knows," he added, with a grin. "Well, what d'you say?"

Anthea clapped her hands in delight.

"Why, that it's the most splendid notion! I declare you're not half so bad an uncle as one's sometimes tempted to think!"

THE END

Other titles in the Ulverscroft Large Print Series:

TO FIGHT THE WILD
Rod Ansell and Rachel Percy

Lost in uncharted Australian bush, Rod Ansell survived by hunting and trapping wild animals, improvising shelter and using all the bushman's skills he knew.

COROMANDEL
Pat Barr

India in the 1830s is a hot, uncomfortable place, where the East India Company still rules. Amelia and her new husband find themselves caught up in the animosities which seethe between the old order and the new.

THE SMALL PARTY
Lillian Beckwith

A frightening journey to safety begins for Ruth and her small party as their island is caught up in the dangers of armed insurrection.

THE WILDERNESS WALK
Sheila Bishop

Stifling unpleasant memories of a misbegotten romance in Cleave with Lord Francis Aubrey, Lavinia goes on holiday there with her sister. The two women are thrust into a romantic intrigue involving none other than Lord Francis.

THE RELUCTANT GUEST
Rosalind Brett

Ann Calvert went to spend a month on a South African farm with Theo Borland and his sister. They both proved to be different from her first idea of them, and there was Storr Peterson — the most disturbing man she had ever met.

ONE ENCHANTED SUMMER
Anne Tedlock Brooks

A tale of mystery and romance and a girl who found both during one enchanted summer.

CLOUD OVER MALVERTON
Nancy Buckingham

Dulcie soon realises that something is seriously wrong at Malverton, and when violence strikes she is horrified to find herself under suspicion of murder.

AFTER THOUGHTS
Max Bygraves

The Cockney entertainer tells stories of his East End childhood, of his RAF days, and his post-war showbusiness successes and friendships with fellow comedians.

MOONLIGHT AND MARCH ROSES
D. Y. Cameron

Lynn's search to trace a missing girl takes her to Spain, where she meets Clive Hendon. While untangling the situation, she untangles her emotions and decides on her own future.